BBC National Short Story Award 2009

BBC National Short Story Award

First published in 2009 by

Short Books

3A Exmouth House

Pine Street

EC1R 0JH

10 9 8 7 6 5 4 3 2 1

A CIP catalogue record for this book
is available from the British Library.

ISBN 978-1-906021-87-0

Contents

Preface
Tom Sutcliffe   7

Other People's Gods
Naomi Alderman   15

The Not-Dead and the Saved
Kate Clanchy   33

Moss Witch
Sara Maitland   57

Hitting Trees with Sticks
Jane Rogers   75

Exchange Rates
Lionel Shriver   91

Biographical Notes   117

Preface

A PAUSE TO reflect on the fallen might be fitting first of all. The attrition was terrible, after all, close to 700 submissions reduced to just 50 by teams of BBC and Booktrust readers before our panel of judges – Helen Dunmore, Will Young, Margaret Drabble, Di Speirs and me – even began work. And then – with a kill rate that makes decimation seem mild – nine out of ten fell to leave this year's shortlist. And none of the standard clichés for this process will quite do justice to what took place. 'Weeding out'? Well, perhaps there were a few weeds amongst the stories that didn't make it through – but there were plenty of orchids too, stories that might well have triumphed if there had been only one or two judges rather than five to please. What about 'distillation' then? That won't do either, given that there was no pure essence towards which we were working. What was boiled off wasn't impurity – because a kind of distinctive impurity was what we were looking for, stories that didn't fit a single literary formula but were uniquely and irreducibly their own thing. And 'whittling down' wouldn't work either – because we weren't carving our way towards some pre-determined shape, but trying to find stories whose voices persisted in the hubbub. In that process a lot of very good stories by very good writers fell by the wayside – but nobody would describe them as off-cuts.

The standard word for such collective decisions is 'consensus' – and it sometimes gets a bad name on occasions like this, as if it automatically reflects a lowest common denominator settlement of dis-agreement. I've sometimes assumed that myself in the past, from the outside of a judging process. But I know it doesn't do justice to our selection here, be-cause before we met to decide on the stories that we wanted to give to a wider audience – through this book and the BBC broadcasts of the shortlist – we each submitted a shortlist of our own, in the dark about the choices of our fellow judges. The degree of overlap was surprising and also gratifying. All of the stories here had multiple votes before the discussions even began – hard evidence that we didn't talk ourselves towards a bearable compromise in that judging session, but rather were bringing a pre-existing agreement into the open. There were, of course, lost causes and rueful acknowledgements that a private enthusiasm hadn't proved contagious. But our final shortlist seemed to us one that we could be proud of – offering a sense of how many different things the short story can do.

Overcoming prejudices is one of those achievements. I have a mild allergy to magical realism and still find it hard to believe that an account of the meeting between a supernatural spirit and a botanist could survive that engrained distaste. But Sara Maitland's tale *MossWitch* managed it, with an exactly judged piece of prose that beautifully captured the ancient panic that very remote and very quiet places can still stir in us. She's spent the last ten years living a happily solitary life in a remote part of Galloway – and you can hear the moorland wind blowing through her story. Lionel Shriver's *Exchange Rates* couldn't present more of a contrast – set in London and beset by everyday urban anxieties – about how to split the bill after a meal with your dad and how to split your belongings when a relationship ends. Like the very first BBC Short Story

Prize winner – James Lasdun's *An Anxious Man* – it charts the varying exchange rates of monetary and emotional values – a reminder that petty cash can get very petty indeed.

The American writer Ambrose Bierce, a skilled short-story writer himself, once pointedly defined the novel as 'a short story padded' – a nice expression of the way in which a good short story limits itself in nothing but word count. In our longlist there were some very fine pieces of writing that we finally set aside because we felt that they were novels in progress rather than short stories achieved; good as they were, they read like extracts of a larger work. But there were also stories that compressed a novel's worth of material into a very small space – such as Kate Clanchy's *The Not-Dead and The Saved*, in which a mother's intense, protective love for her terminally ill son finds itself expressed in sometimes startling ways. And there were stories that brought a deceptive lightness to difficult and familiar subjects. Jane Rogers' *Hitting Trees With Sticks* doesn't describe the confusions of age from the outside – it enacts them, with such deftness that even on a second reading you can't be quite sure whether it's the narrator that is at an odd angle to the world or the other way round. And to complete our shortlist we chose *Other People's Gods*, a deceptively innocent story by Naomi

Alderman, which tackles the weighty and substantial themes of faith and respect with a winning humour.

In *Ulysses* James Joyce famously had Leopold Bloom put a short story to brusquely lavatorial use. Taking a copy of *Titbits* into the jakes, Bloom looks for something 'new and easy' and finds *Matcham's Masterstroke*, rewarded by the publishers at a rate of a guinea a column. 'It did not move or touch him,' he concludes, 'but it was something quick and neat.' Then, reading on 'above his own rising smell', he notes approvingly that it 'begins and ends morally'. Tearing half the sheet away, he then employs it in a way that no author would ever want for their work. Our short-story writers might envy the comparatively lavish remuneration Mr Philip Beaufoy receives and the fact that a popular magazine was in the market for short stories – which is very rarely the case now. But they can take some satisfaction in the fact that Bloom's description is as far from the truth about their own work as it's possible to get. These stories *did* move and touch us – and their relative brevity – in word count – had no bearing on how they lasted in the mind. They demonstrate what should scarcely need proving any more – that the short story isn't a disposable genre, there to fill a gap too narrow for a novel. It's a form which, at its best, has a weight entirely at odds with its mass.

We hope you enjoy these ones just as much as we did when we made our selection, and that they pique an appetite to read more. If the judging process brought home anything to us it was that shortlists are always too short.

Tom Sutcliffe

Other People's Gods
Naomi Alderman

MR BLOOM LED a blameless life until he saw Ganesha. Some people do. Some, like Mr Bloom, go to ophthalmic college at their mother's insistence although in their hearts they had yearned to travel to far-off lands. Some, like him, dream of spice islands and dusky maidens but settle for Telma stock cubes and the buxom daughter of the retiring optician, Mr Lefkowitz. Some, like Mr Bloom, raise a family and examine rheumy eyes and rub their corns at night and quite forget in all that piling-up of years that once they longed to stand bare-chested on a shore of golden sand, to go where man had never trod, to love as man had never loved. Some find contentment there, and others discontent. Mr Bloom, quite to his own surprise, found Ganesha.

He was on a market stall, among bangles and saris, joss sticks and wall hangings. There, in the centre, a porcelain statue of a four-armed man with an elephant's head, or perhaps an elephant with the body of a four-armed man. He was bright pink, with large kind eyes and a golden headdress. One of his hands was beckoning, another motioning the observer to stay away. Mr Bloom saw at once that this was a god; what else could it be, enticing and warning at the same moment? He picked up the statue, the glaze smooth beneath his fingertips. The young man tending the stall, dirty blond dreadlocks falling into his eyes, said:

'Careful, Grandpa, yeah? You break it, you pay, alright?'

Mr Bloom thought of the story of Abraham our forefather, who condemned his father for *avodah zara*, by which is meant foreign worship, by which is meant idol worship. As a young boy, realising the truth that there is only one God, Abraham smashed his father's idols. When his father punished him, Abraham said, 'No, father, it wasn't me, it was the biggest idol. He took a stick and smashed all the others.' His father said, 'You idiot, idols can't move!' and Abraham replied, 'So why do you worship them, then?' The story does not relate whether at that moment Abraham's father was enlightened, or whether, on the contrary, he punished Abraham yet harder for stripping him of the beliefs which, in prehistoric Mesopotamia, must have been even more precious than they are today.

Mr Bloom considered all this as he held Ganesha in his hands. Those eyes were so tender, full of love for whatever they looked upon. Those arms were so strong; with him on one's side how could a person ever fail? Mr Bloom had never touched an idol before, never before considered that the sin of *avodah zara* could have any practical application. He looked at the smooth curl of the trunk, mighty yet comforting.

'I'll take him,' he said.

For a while, Mr Bloom thought he could hide Ganesha. He wrapped the god in plastic bags, cushioned him with hundreds of soft lens-cleaning cloths, and tucked him behind the stack of Passover dishes at the bottom of the wardrobe in the spare room. But it was no use. Somehow his wife always seemed to need something from right at the back of that very wardrobe and he was sent to retrieve it. Or one of his children would have left the door open. Whenever Mr Bloom went near the spare room, Ganesha's trunk would have worked its way out of its wrapping and waved at him, bold and pink, from the plastic-bag swaddling.

He wants to be worshipped, thought Mr Bloom,

and knew at once that it was true, for wasn't that always what gods wanted? Love and gifts, or fear and wars, or sometimes both. But how to worship him? Mr Bloom was puzzled; he had never worshipped an idol before, and had not the least idea of the proper way to do so. He looked in his Bible. 'Thou shalt not make for thyself graven images,' he read. 'Thou shalt not bow down to them or worship them.' Then, later, God said 'an altar shalt thou make for me, and sacrifice thereon thy burnt offerings, thy sheep and thine oxen'. Mr Bloom had neither sheep nor oxen, and did not particularly want to make a burnt offering of his professional equivalent. He had once melted a pair of spectacles by mistake and the fumes had been revolting. But bowing down and worshipping seemed fairly easy to achieve.

Mr Bloom placed Ganesha on a raffia footstool in the spare room, taking care to close the door first. Ganesha seemed happy, the fiery glint in his eye now one of deep approval. Slowly, mindful of the mild arthritis in his right knee, Mr Bloom lowered himself to the floor, then bowed so that his forehead touched the ground.

'O Great Ganesha,' he intoned, in a prayer he had composed himself, 'I humbly thank you for gracing my home with your presence. I pray, O lord Ganesha, that you will bless all those who dwell here. And I especially beseech you, all-knowing and most merciful Ganesha, to help my daughter Judy in her law Alevel for, O kind Ganesha, she finds the coursework very hard to understand. Ohhhhh mighty Ganesha,' he said, attempting to raise himself up into a kneeling position again, to proceed with his prayer. But though his spirit longed to give Ganesha due praise, Mr Bloom's back was weak. A muscle in his left buttock spasmed, he crouched down again and, waiting for the pain to subside, it was in this position that his wife found him twenty minutes later.

'Reuben!' she said. 'What in God's name do you think you're doing?'

'I,' he said, 'Sandra, my back, it's gone again, bring the Deep Heat!' He hoped to distract her long enough to crawl with Ganesha to the wardrobe and conceal him, but Sandra was more sharp-witted than that.

'Reuben!' she said again, 'is that an *idol*? Were you *worshipping* an *idol* in our own home, with me so busy with the Pesach cleaning and the Rabbi coming for lunch on Shabbes?'

'Sandra!' Mr Bloom replied. 'How can you say such a thing?' For Mr Bloom hadn't been married for twenty years without learning a thing or two himself. 'No,' he continued, 'I found this *statue* on a market stall and I thought it might suit the colour scheme in this room.' Mrs Bloom had nagged him for years to take a greater interest in such domestic matters. 'I was just... examining it when I tripped and fell and hurt my back.'

'Hmmm,' said Sandra.

'Deep Heat?' said Mr Bloom. 'Please, my love?'

Sandra, whose heart was kind although her tongue was sharp, hurried to the bathroom to fetch the tube of healing ointment.

In the meantime, Mr Bloom attempted, without a great deal of success, to replace the statue of Ganesha in his wrappings, to cover over his flamboyance and thus cease to distress his wife. But the trunk seemed unaccountably slippery, and the bubble wrap must have shrunk a little. When Sandra returned, Ganesha was still sitting on the floor. She massaged the soothing cream deep into her husband's buttock while staring thoughtfully at the god. At last, her fingers still menthol-fragrant, she picked up the statue and examined it critically.

'Do you know,' she said, 'I think it might do for the living room. On the sideboard. It's very ethnic.'

And so Ganesha took up residence at the very centre of the Bloom home. The children objected naturally, as children always do.

'Errrr,' said Judy at breakfast, while munching her Marmite bagel, 'I think it's staring at me.'

'Yuck,' said David, flicking Ganesha with his fingernail as he hoisted his schoolbag. 'It looks dirty. I bet it's infested.'

'The statue is hollow,' said Mr Bloom mildly, wondering in his heart why God chose to turn delightful babies into charmless teenagers, 'and his name is Ganesha.'

David rolled his eyes. Judy sighed. They went to school. As Mr Bloom was taking the breakfast dishes into the kitchen he paused for a moment in front of Ganesha, inclined his head slightly, and left a morsel of bagel on a saucer in front of him.

Mr Bloom could not help but notice that his life seemed better with Ganesha in it. When Mrs Rosenblatt, of the Rosenblatt Dried Fruit empire, missed her fourth appointment in a row, Mr Bloom did not tremble at the idea of rebuking her. Instead, he felt a mastery, a calmness, a purposeful strength. He picked up the telephone without hesitation and said:

'Mrs Rosenblatt, your appointment has now been rescheduled for half past four. If you are not in my shop at half past four, Bloom's Opticians will have no further need of your custom.'

'But...' said Mrs Rosenblatt.

'No further need,' he said again.

'But Mr...' said Mrs Rosenblatt.

'Thank you,' said Mr Bloom, 'and good day.'

Mrs Rosenblatt appeared, punctual and meek, at half past four. As Mr Bloom ushered her into his eye-testing room he muttered a quiet prayer of thanks to Ganesha.

The rest of the family, too, grew increasingly fond of the god as the days went on. Ganesha's gaze was so magnanimous, he filled the living room with a sense of quiet peace. Mr Bloom noticed that Sandra and Judy and David spent longer in that room now. David took to doing his homework on the table under the watching eye of Ganesha. And Mr Bloom noticed that, though Judy was still dismissive and disdainful of the statue, on the morning before her module exam she left a badge from her jacket on the sideboard in front of him. She caught her father's eye as she turned to go, shrugged uncomfortably and said: 'For luck. You know.' And when Judy did better in that examination than in her teachers' opinions she had any right to, Ganesha came to be looked on in the Bloom family home with a certain warmth.

At first, the Blooms did not speak of Ganesha outside their home. But Hendon is not a place for secrets. Perhaps it was that Judy's friend from school, Mikaella, observed her placing a small handful of yellow mandel croutons in front of the god before she started her homework. Perhaps it was that

David's friend Benjy wondered why David rubbed the statue's head before the final round of every Wii Tennis game. However it happened, soon one person spoke to another and another to a third and it became known in Hendon that the Blooms – yes, Bloom's the optician, yes, Sandra Bloom of the PTA, yes, that nice David Bloom whose barmitzvah they'd attended only two short years before – those very Blooms had an idol in their house.

Now, it is made very clear in the Bible that the introduction of idolatry into a good Jewish home cannot go unchallenged. Were not 3,000 men put to death for worshipping a golden calf? And was it not for this very sin of idolatry that Jezebel was thrown from a window to be devoured by wild dogs? Of course, Barnet Council would be much alarmed should such events come to pass in Hendon. And thus it was that Mr Bloom was not awakened in the night by a party of eunuchs come to effect his defenestration, but instead received a telephone call asking that he should kindly pay a visit to the Rabbi at his earliest convenience.

The Rabbi was a young man, only recently finished with his seminary education. Nonetheless, his beard was neat and his manner suitably deferential to a man of Mr Bloom's seniority.

'Now, aheheh,' he said, steepling his fingers, 'I

wanted to talk to you, Mr Bloom, about your, um, statue.'

'Oh yes?' said Mr Bloom. He did not feel perturbed. He had found that since Ganesha had entered his life, he had been less easily disturbed by all vicissitudes. He felt solid.

'Yes,' said the Rabbi. He fiddled with his beard nervously. 'The thing is, Mr Bloom, there's been talk. That is, there has started to be talk. Not, you understand, that I listen to talk, no, not at all, but a man of your position, a trustee of the synagogue, Mr Bloom...'

'Talk?' said Mr Bloom, mildly.

'About your statue, Mr Bloom. People are talking about your statue.' The Rabbi began to speak more quickly, clearly discomfited by Mr Bloom's silence. 'The thing is, Mr Bloom, it doesn't do for a synagogue trustee to have a... to have a...'

'A god?' Mr Bloom volunteered.

'An idol,' said the Rabbi. 'It doesn't do for someone in your position to have an idol in your house. So, um, get rid of it, please.'

Mr Bloom thought about how his house had changed since the arrival of Ganesha. It was not, of course, that the family was unrecognizable. Not that there was no longer any strife or bitterness. They continued to argue, to complain; things continued to go wrong. And yet, the quiet presence of the elephant-headed god seemed to have strengthened each of them. Perhaps, thought Mr Bloom, it was his imagination. And yet he would rather not give the god up.

'I think,' he said, 'that I would rather not.'

The Rabbi frowned and leaned forward in his chair, earnest and sincere.

'Now look here, Mr Bloom,' he said, 'we can both be reasonable about this, can't we? Of course you know and I know that you don't *worship* the thing. But can't you see that it looks all wrong?'

'But I do,' said Mr Bloom.

'Ah,' said the Rabbi, satisfied, 'at least you can see that.'

'No,' said Mr Bloom, 'I mean that I do worship him.'

And the Rabbi sat back suddenly as if Mr Bloom, the kindly optician, had struck him in the face.

'Hmm,' he said after a long pause, 'we should talk more. Perhaps tomorrow?'

On the second day, the Rabbi telephoned in the afternoon and invited Mr Bloom to come to talk with him in his study at the synagogue.

'Mr Bloom,' said the Rabbi, obviously a little nervous, 'I want to talk to you about God.'

Mr Bloom smiled and said, 'that's your field,

Rabbi, not mine.'

The Rabbi smiled thinly, 'Quite, quite. But the thing is, Mr Bloom, God is really quite specific about idols. Second commandment, you know. No other gods before me. Make for yourself no graven image. It's really very clear.'

Mr Bloom nodded slowly.

'I don't see how you can say that you "worship" a statue and still keep your place on the synagogue board, you see, Mr Bloom. I don't see how we can keep on letting you attend the synagogue at all.'

Mr Bloom said, mildly, 'But I still keep the laws. I still pray to God. I'm still a Jew.'

And the Rabbi spread his hands wide and smiled nervously and shook his head and said: 'Ah, but "I the Lord your God am a jealous God," you know.'

Mr Bloom thought of Ganesha, his wide, kind eyes, his welcoming arms. 'If God is so great,' he said, 'why is he jealous? I thought we weren't supposed to covet.'

And the Rabbi's face darkened, and he said: 'I can see we will have to talk further about this, Mr Bloom.'

And on the third day, Mr Bloom received another telephone call. It was in the early morning; Mr Bloom's shop was not due to open for another hour. The Rabbi apologized for calling so early and said: 'Mr Bloom. I have thought a great deal about what you have said. I think I should see the statue for myself. I wonder if you would be able to bring it here, to the synagogue, this morning? I think that the whole matter could be resolved if you would bring the statue here.'

Mr Bloom agreed that he would do so. He had, after all, benefited a great deal from the synagogue and its Rabbis. He was still a Jew. Whatever arguments the Rabbi might wish to muster, he, Bloom, felt honour-bound to hear out.

Mr Bloom wrapped Ganesha in a soft blanket and placed him into a sturdy holdall. As he did so, he caressed the curled trunk reverently. He wondered if, like the prophet Elisha, the Rabbi intended to challenge Ganesha to a duel with the Almighty, Lord of Hosts. He was intrigued to see which god would prevail.

The Rabbi was waiting for Mr Bloom at the synagogue gates. The building was old and respectable. Constructed in the 1920s, its solid bricks had housed generations of prayer, of lamentation and of joyful song. The Rabbi led Mr Bloom through the corridors of the synagogue, not into the main prayer hall, but up via a winding cedar-scented staircase to the choir stalls, perched high above the Holy Closet in which the scrolls of the Torah reside. From here they could look across the ranged ranks of seats in the synagogue, those same seats which filled every Friday and Saturday with hundreds of Jews, come to worship the one and only God.

The Rabbi threw the windows at the back of the choir stalls open, inhaled deeply several times and then turned to Mr Bloom. 'Have you brought the idol?' he asked. Mr Bloom noticed that the Rabbi, too, seemed stronger and less nervous.

Mr Bloom nodded.

'Show him to me,' said the Rabbi.

Mr Bloom withdrew the god from the holdall, unwrapped the soft blanket and held him gently. He thought that perhaps the god was heavier now than when he had bought him.

The Rabbi's nose wrinkled in disgust. 'Do you not know, Mr Bloom, that this thing was made by men? That it is only china and paint? How can you give your worship to something that you could construct yourself?'

Mr Bloom shrugged. It seemed impossible to explain if the Rabbi could not understand it. At last, in an attempt to answer, he said: 'I followed my heart and my eyes,' but thought that this did not explain one tenth of what he hoped to communicate.

The Rabbi looked at Mr Bloom for a long moment. Then, with a little smile, he tugged on Mr

Bloom's arm and brought him to stand by the window too. The synagogue is at the top of a rise, and the whole of Hendon can be seen from its windows, if one is able to peer through the stained glass.

'Mr Bloom,' said the Rabbi, 'I hope you know that God loves you.'

Bloom nodded silently. He gazed upon the contemplative and peaceful face of Ganesha.

'I have never encountered a case such as this,' said the Rabbi. 'I had to consult with the most senior authorities for a ruling.'

Bloom nodded again.

'They were of one mind. You must understand, Mr Bloom, that this is for your own good,' said the Rabbi. Then, in one fluid motion, too quickly for Mr Bloom to react, the Rabbi grabbed Ganesha from Mr Bloom's hands. He held him for a moment, clutching the god close to his body in an almost protective gesture and then hurled him in a wide arc through the synagogue window. With a crisply crunching report, Ganesha smashed into a thousand pieces on the paved area below.

'Now, Mr Bloom,' said the Rabbi beaming, 'don't you feel better, rid of that revolting thing?'

Bloom said nothing. He stared down at the paved courtyard of the synagogue, where bright pink and gold fragments radiated from the central point of impact. At length, he allowed the Rabbi to lead him away from the window and back to his own home.

Late that night, Mr Bloom – who had been synagogue treasurer for many years and remained a keyholder of the building – silently let himself in through the iron gate of the courtyard. He had brought a fine-haired clothesbrush and a carved wooden box from his living room, along with a bag slung over his shoulder containing one or two other, heavier items. Slowly, working in circles, he brushed the dust of Ganesha into the box and, when he was finished, dug a small hole in one of the ornamental flower beds and buried it. He wondered if he should say a few words over the grave, but could think of none that might be appropriate.

Then, still moving without sound, he opened the door to the main building of the synagogue and slipped through. He had rarely been in this vaulted space alone at night, and never without a specific and necessary errand. He paused now, thinking of the many hours of quiet contemplation this place had afforded him, of the services he had heard intoned here, of the comradely chats, the bustling ceremonial, the joyful celebrations and the sombre days.

The next morning, the synagogue officials were startled to find the building not only locked but its locks stuffed with wax. Fearing the worst, they called a locksmith who, after some effort, managed to remove the locks bodily from the doors. The officials – and, by now, a small crowd who had heard that something might be going on at the synagogue – entered and looked around with horror.

The synagogue was ruined. The benches were smashed, the drapery torn, the candlesticks twisted, the windows broken. And in the centre was Mr Bloom, standing with an axe by his side and perspiration soaking through his clothes.

And they said, 'Why have you done this thing?'

And he said, 'I? I? I did not do this. This was done by the Almighty.'

And they looked around again at the benches with the axe-shaped cuts deeply incised into them, and at the places where the upholstery had been ripped out in quantities the size of a man's hand.

And they said, 'God did not do this! God cannot destroy in this way.'

And he said, 'Then why do you worship Him?'

But it is not recorded whether the people were grateful for this enlightenment.

The Not-Dead and the Saved
Kate Clanchy

Not Dead

THEY'VE BEEN ASKED to wait in *Paediatrics*. It is five o'clock, already; and the sun is streaming in through the high, unopenable windows. There's a concert going on in the Day Room: hrum, thrum, thrum, *and his name is Aitken Drum*.

The Son is lying on top of the blanket and has kept his trainers on. He has lately taken to wearing aggressively small jeans which he buys in the children's department and customises with razor blades, black thread and biro drawings in the style of Aubrey Beardsley. He taps his dirty fingers on his ripped tee-shirt. His large, glittering brown eyes sweep the empty ward.

'Look,' he says, in his new, adolescent, scratchy

voice, 'a Not-Dead.'

'What?' says the Mother, sleepily. The Mother has been putting off her tiredness for so long that it tends, like a neglected middle child, to leap at her at the least chance. Just now it is sitting on her lap, arms tight around her neck, breathing the scents of *Paediatrics* into her mouth: strawberry syrup, toasted cheese, pee.

'A Not-Dead,' says the Son. 'Look. Under the window.'

Mother cranes round, then stands up briefly. She sees a baby sleeping in a plastic cot. It is wearing a pink woolly hat and cardigan and has oxygen tubes in its nose.

'See,' says the Son.

'It's a baby,' says the Mother, crossly, 'some-one's baby.' But the baby's eyes are too far apart, and it has a cleft palate, and its whole body has a flattened, spatch-cocked look, as if it is trying to separate into two pieces, East and West, and the Mother is already worrying that there might be a crisis and she will be called upon to Do Some-thing. The Mother is not a good choice for the parent of a chronic invalid. She is scrawny and im-patient and she fears sick things: fallen fledglings, wounds, things that pulse. Someone else always has to pick them up. Her ex-husband preferably, who is bluff and easy with illness, who would carry the Son, as a six-year-old, casually around the hospital in his arms, the tubes draped jokily but handily over his shoulders – talents he is now wasting on a new, completely well, wife and child.

'She should be dead,' says the Son, 'like in nature. I mean if that baby was born in a primitive tribe she'd be dead in seconds.'

'So would lots of people,' says the Mother. 'So would I.'

'I would,' says the Son. 'Definitely.' He raises his fists to his forehead, surveys the puncture wounds inside his elbows, and adds, 'I'd be the deadest.' The Mother feels impatient. Once, the Son was prodigious and original, and the Mother was daffy and whacky, and they were on the same side: now they seem doomed to partake in endless EFL oral exams, with the Son taking the part of the difficult student, the one with the nose stud.

'You were a perfectly healthy baby,' she snaps.

'Not really,' says the Son. 'Only *apparently*. I was born with it, remember. My tumour. That's what the new guy reckons.' Oncology is a new favourite subject. So is genetics, and blame. The Mother decides not to meet the Son's eye.

'Anyway,' she says instead, 'we're not primitive.'

'No,' says the Son, leaning back on his pillows,

'we've got the technology now. And cos we have the technology, we have to save her. The baby. I mean the Doctors and people, when a baby like that is born, they have to save her. It would be <u>wrong</u> to ask them not to save her, I can totally see that, cos then they would be like murderers.'

'And?' says the Mother.

'So then the person they save is not dead, but sometimes they're not alive either. Like they need the technology to keep them going? Like they can't be properly alive, but no one knows what to do with them? Not Dead. See?'

The Mother wakes up. She scents danger. She leans forward, and the Son fixes her with his shining eyes.

'I see them everywhere. You know? Not just in the hospital. Some of them are in disguise, but I can spot them. Like they have a little shiny outline round them, like in a game on a screen. They pixelate, Mum, they pixelate at me. Like: there, there, there. Shouldn't really be here. You, you, you. Not really here. Me, me, me. Not-Dead.'

'No,' says the Mother, loudly, unsurely, 'you're alive.'

'I'm not dead,' says the Son, 'because of the Machine, but where am I alive?'

'In your mind,' says the Mother, 'you're alive in

your mind, that's the thing. The life of the mind.'

Because the Mother believes this most sincerely. And so, during the long while they have to wait for the plasma and the trolley, for the Machine and the nurses, the Mother babbles about Robert Louis Stevenson, also sickly, also bookish. Then she enumerates to the Son the titles of all the books he loves the most, all the books they've read together, their favourite episodes, and, after a while, the Son says, 'You know *White Fang*? I was thinking about that. I think it's like a prequel to *Call of the Wild*. White Fang is Buck's grandfather. You can work it out. There are, like, all these little clues.'

Then he curls down on the pillows, and chatters on about the great dog Buck, and how he is actually fulfilling White Fang's dream or maybe, like, the call of his *genes* when he runs into oblivion in the Canadian woods, and daringly the mother takes his hand and folds it inside her own and remembers how soft it was when he was a little boy, really as soft as a petal, the curved veined petal of a magnolia in its brief springtime brilliance; and all the while the baby breathes in its tubing, its arms abandoned by its sides, its ribcage moving up and down with exaggerated depth in its pink covers, like a giant, disconnected, heart.

Three weeks later, they are in *Acute General*.

They can't be in a single room, because of the price of nurses. Because nurses have to watch him, now. Because, yesterday, the Son unplugged his Machine and watched silently as his life blood was pumped to the floor. And where was his Mother? His Mother was on her way to the library, that's where, because her Son had said, 'Go and find a job, a life of your own,' that's why. She was more than halfway there when she turned and sprinted back. She doesn't know why.

Now they have pumped pints of blood back into his veins, now they have reinflated his internal organs and wheeled him out of the ICU. Now the Mother and Son are going to have their first conversation. The tubes are out of his throat, but they seem to be in hers. She feels as if she has a broomstick stuffed in her mouth. They need to have this conversation. There is morphine still in his system, she should remember. They are in a bay with the curtains drawn. Acute General. Anyone could overhear.

'It was an impulse, Mum,' he says, loudly, to the ceiling tiles, his voice hoarser than ever. 'One of those things. Try not to fixate, okay?'

'How can it be an impulse,' hisses the Mother, furiously, round the broomstick, 'to bypass six security systems?'

'Oh, I worked out how to do that ages ago,'

carols the Son. 'Sort of for the fun of it. Like chess. You know?'

The Mother taught the Son to play chess herself. He is a ferocious player, but he fastens too fixedly on elaborate schemes, seven-move tangos of knights and rooks, and cries when he realises he has left his king unguarded, mate in two. Yes, she can see how he could do that: work it all out. And already, just two moves in, the Mother starts to weep, and the Son looks at her, then away.

'The thing is, Mum,' says the Son, picking his nails, 'you got it wrong.'

The Mother is prepared to accept she has got many things wrong. Which one, though?

'Robert Louis Stevenson?' says the Son. 'Remember? He just wasn't that ill, Robert Louis Stevenson. He could walk. He got to have sex. He grew fucking up, Mum. Not –' the boy gestures at his feet, sticking up in a little tent of blanket halfway down the bed.

The Mother slumps out of her chair and puts her head on the end of the bed, on the brown hairy hospital blanket. She is thinking about her love for her son. It was born at the same time as him, and she is not in control of it. She imagines it as very strong and not at all intelligent, something that moves about in the dark and grabs things. It has claws and tiny eyes, like a lobster. The mother decides to say something stupid, so as not to go on thinking:

'But your transplant,' says the Mother, 'it could be any time. Next month.'

'Yeah,' says the Son, 'exactly.' And they both remember the last transplant.

'What about me?' says the Mother, after a while, sitting back on her heels. 'What would I do without you? How would I feel?'

The Son sighs deeply. 'Mum,' he says, 'you have to see, don't you? You have to see that I can't be responsible for that?'

Paediatrics, again. They've been called in for the transplant, but there's been an emergency, and a blood test gone AWOL, and here is the upshot: wait overnight. The Mother doesn't mind: she knows the ward so well, and how to change the sofa into a bed. She is doing that, and the Son is lying on the bed, plugged into his i-pod and a drip-stand, when he takes out his ear piece and beckons to her conspiratorially.

'Look,' he whispers, 'it's the Not-Dead baby.'

The Mother sits by him on the bed and peers where he points, out through the gap in the curtains. In the opposite bay, flanked by machinery, is a cot and a pink-clad shape.

'Are you sure,' says the Mother, 'it's the same one? That was months ago. Wouldn't she have grown?'

'Mum,' says the Son, 'haven't you learnt anything? Of course she wouldn't grow.' Now a woman stands up, and draws the curtains of the bay. In the slice of light they glimpse the shadow of her belly.

'I hope she didn't see us,' says the Mother.

'Did you see her?' hisses the Son. 'Pregnant! Holey moley!' and he collapses theatrically flat against his pillows. The Mother finishes pulling out her sofa bed and lies on it. It is incredibly narrow: her elbows are on wood. Her Son is staring at the ceiling, and has not replugged the i-pod.

'Is it bad that she's pregnant?' she says, after a while. In *Paediatrics*, there are pictures on the ceiling: Piglet and Pooh, walking into the sunset.

'No,' says the Son, 'but it's weird.'

'How weird?'

'Well, that baby is going to die. The Not-Dead one. I think it has Edwards Syndrome. I looked it up. So that baby will die, and then, just at the same time, she'll have a new baby. And then what will they think?'

'Maybe,' says the Mother, though it is a bothering thought, 'they'll think they've got a new baby to love?'

'Yeah, and maybe they'll think the old baby got a new body? You know? Transmutation of souls?'

'Would that be bad?'

'Not like, Hitler bad, but it is fucked up. Because, what I think is, your soul doesn't exist. Your mind doesn't, even. Your mind is a bit of your body. It's just the same. That's what the Prozac tells you, Mum. See. Look at us. We've taken the pills, and they've changed our bodies, and that's changed our minds. Here we are, having the transplant, happy campers. Different souls. See?'

'Yes,' says the Mother, who has brought zopiclone with her and is about to take one, 'I do see that. I see that point.'

'I'm going to put the light out now,' says the Son, and does. In the dark he says, in his dalek voice from way back, from his Doctor Who phase, 'Tomorrow, I get my transplant. Then, I start to grow. I am on drugs that make me optimistic, so this is easy. Good night, mother-unit.'

The Mother's pillow smells of rubber. The wall next to her head is padded vinyl. When the Son was little, she would lie here and tell him they were camping out, in the Dormobile, lost in the French countryside. She tries to tell herself one of these stories now, but can only think of the Son's illness, the long road, the many forks, and how, at each one, they have borne inexplicably left, further and further down B routes, nearer and nearer the sea. Recently, several people have told her that the Son owes her his life, but the Mother doesn't feel that at all. It is she who owes him his, in the same way you owe a child a good picnic, when it is your idea to set out, and you who forgot the map, and now you are lost and there is no hope ever of the rain turning off.

A Spike on the Graph

This is a new hospital, in the city where the Son now goes to University. The Mother had to get a taxi and a plane and another taxi; she had to ask at two reception desks; a junior Doctor met her at the second and is now trotting beside her; he is saying the crisis has peaked, and new antibiotics and best foot forward, hopefully; but she can hardly hear him for the fire-doors and steel barriers swing-swinging in her head; but here they are: *Cardio-Respiratory*.

The Son is already stable. He is sitting up in bed, attached to, for him, a minor amount of apparatus. He will always be small, but his cheekbones are good, he is bonily handsome. 'Lollypop head,' he says, of himself. 'I should be on TV.' There are girls, now, and here is one beside him, importantly holding his hand. She has blond hair in plaits and liquid dark eyes and an animated, elegant, deer-like way of holding her head and back.

'Oh!' cries the Girl, in a sweet, carrying voice. 'Look, here you are! He's come through! He's beaten the infection back! They never saw such a spike on the graph!'

The Mother sinks on to the edge of the bed, her mouth open, her hands stretched out, her body pulsing forward, ga-ga-ga-ga, my dearest love, and the Son gives her a quick lift of the eyebrow and an embarrassed smile. He lifts his hand but it is encumbered with tubes and with the girl's hand. He is about to drop out of college and marry the girl; he is going to live on an organic farm with a white-robed group of medical emergency survivors called The Saved he is going to give up meat, alcohol and irony and assume white robes and quasi-Zen belief; he is going to surrender to the leadership of a tall, wintery, ex-kidney patient named Attila, and he will tell his mother that he is dedicated to the celebration of the moment and meditation and macrobiotics and this is why she cannot visit him or speak on the phone or even write more than twice a year, and, that all this is done with his free will and is legal and not a cult and that Attila has plenty of experience with private detectives and the resulting period of constant acute tension and mourning will last more than three years; and though his gesture may start as an embrace, it ends as a flat-handed, Popish, stop-sign.

Saved

A third hospital. This ward is *Acute Assessment*. Here is the Mother who has just sat down, and here is the Wife on the opposite chair, wearing grubby white cheesecloth robes with a blue cardigan over them and chewing a bead of her amber necklace. The Son is propped up on pillows with his eyes shut. His hair has come out in tufts, now, and his skin is yellow-green and mottled like slipware. Now he is thin as a November guy.

The Son opens his eyes. Something has happened to them: they have curdled or solidified, gone from beer, full of yellow lights, to toffee. It must be the Wife's fault. The Son doesn't greet the Mother. He says to her:

'It's the baby. I can't stand the baby.'

'What do you mean?' says the Mother, 'What baby?'

'His baby,' says the Wife, pointing to a toddler playing in a shaft of sunlight on the other side of the ward. The child is also wearing white – a dirty little tee-shirt and a hefty covered nappy – and the light catches the filaments of his hair. The trout, love, thrashes in the Grandmother's chest.

'He wants juice,' says the Son. 'Then he wants milk. Then he spills it on the floor. Then he howls. I mean, is that reasonable? Does it strike you as reasonable behaviour?'

'When did you have the Baby?' says the Mother.

'Don't you mean why?' says the Son. The Son has broken out in a sweat, the beads standing out on his yellow skin. His sharp limbs twitch under the sheet.

'He's fourteen months,' says the Wife, taking the bead out of her mouth. 'He was born at the farm. A water birth.' She makes a calm blank face and looks straight at the Mother, her eyes so wide apart they could have a blind spot between them like a cat's.

'I'm taking Jaybird back to the Farm now. Ok?' she says. But the Son has his eyes shut. The Mother runs after the Wife, and at the Ward door she puts her hand briefly on the Baby's head and tries to smile at the Wife, but it comes out as a moan.

The Son opens his eyes for his mother. 'They think I have a brain tumour,' he says. 'They're really pretty sure. Maybe even more than one brain tumour, they're going to do a scan. Then they might want to do chemo but I can't be bothered, I mean what's the point, do you think?'

'Is that why you're angry with the baby?' said the Mother. She knows this doesn't come first, but the heat of the Baby's head is still burning in her palm.

'How should I know?' said the Son. 'How can any-one know that, Mum?' And then he vomits on the floor, and fits, and his Mother, still squeamish after all these years, doesn't know where to touch him and jumps up and shudders and finally presses the alarm above the bed and the Doctors come, dozens of them, more than even she has ever seen.

In *Oncology,* the Mother is shown images of the tumours. There are three: bore holes or storm systems or black beetles in the bright contour maps of her son's brain, and the Consultant wants to oper-ate or at the very least shrink them with chemo or radio. The Son is refusing all treatment, but, as the Consultant says, the tumours are already actively disturbing the state of the Son's mind, and so perhaps he should be Sectioned.

'No,' says the Son, to the Consultant, 'this is really me. This is actually how angry I am. I am actu-ally this angry with hospitals. I really do hate you. You are not doing anyone any good and I do not give you permission to put your fingers in my brain.'

But it is true he is also angry with everyone else. He can't remember why he asked his Mother to come, and keeps shouting for her to be taken away. When Attila arrives, in his clean white nightie, carry-ing Tupperware boxes, the Son refuses to let him lay on hands, and calls the proffered macrobiotic curry a 'cow-pat'. The Mother, watching from the next bay, smirks, and in a whirl of white, Attila catches her arm in his hairy hand.

'I'm going to tell you a story,' he says, as the Mother blinks into his large-boned, plain face. 'About laughing. My *roshi* had a tumour in his arm. He watched it grow, and he said to it, "Tumour, you will be the death of me". And then he laughed at the tumour. At first, we could not understand, but then we laughed with him, and after some days of laughing the tumour shrank and disappeared. I saw this with my own eyes. Now, laughing woman, will you laugh with me?' The Mother is shaking her head but Attila opens his big bearded mouth and laughs, mirthlessly and loudly, showing his teeth, big as a donkey's.

'Holey moley,' says the Son, and pulls his blanket over his head.

This, to the Mother, demonstrates that the Son is sane. But next, in comes the Wife, with the Baby, and the Son turns his back on them and buries himself in his pillow, and when the Baby tries to tug it off with his little plump hands, calling 'funny dada', the Mother witnesses the Son knock the child over on the lino, and in the stramash that follows, the screaming, fits and forcible injections, she thinks the small cold thought that perhaps the Son should be Sectioned, after all.

The Mother sits by the Son's bed while he sleeps. When he wakes, his eyes are clear.

'You were right,' says the Son. 'We shouldn't have had him.'

'I didn't say that,' she replies. 'How could I? I wasn't there.'

'You didn't need to be,' he says. 'I internalised your response.'

It is indecent, how much this pleases her.

'But you love him,' she says, hopefully, 'the baby?'

'I expect so,' says the Son, 'but I'm letting him down. You see?'

'Yes,' says the Mother. 'It's a terrible feeling.' But the Mother is smiling, because she is still looking into her boy's eyes. Over the years, she has lived with many imaginary versions of the Son – a spry, unmarried one, most recently, but also a heavy-limbed footballing boy, also a big lad who picks up her bags at the station, easily, as if they were empty, also a grown man who lifts her off her feet, tight to his cashmere chest, and all of them have had these eyes, eyes with gold lights, with pinpoints of the true dear dark.

'Because this time,' says the Son, 'I am going to die. And you have to let me. You really do.'

In the Hospice, the tumours eat the Son's brain rapidly, like chalk cliffs eroding in a storm. Things fall
off: houses, people. So, when the Wife comes in, the
Son turns to her and smiles, and her face opens in
joy.

'Hello,' says the Son. 'Have you come to visit me?'

'I brought Jaybird,' she says, indicating the child.

'Is he yours?' he says.

It takes a further fifteen minutes of conversation – during which the Mother gets to play
peekaboo with the Baby, the sweetness of which she
will remember all her life – to truly establish that
the Son has no recollection of ever having met the
Wife or the Baby, but that he thinks them interest-
ing and pretty. The Wife leaves the hospital at once,
the Baby like a luggage on her shoulder, and gets in a
taxi, the Mother at her side all the way, pleading. 'It
isn't you he's forgotten,' says the Wife, and the Mother feels a goldfish flick of pleasure.

Now they are in the *Garden Wing*, which is not
for *Respite*. The tumours are busy, eating words.
They substitute 'sausage' for bedpan and 'window'
for drink, but for a long time they are unable to
eat music. So, round the Son, everyone sings 'I
love coffee' or hums 'Food, glorious food'.

One night, the tumours have swallowed fifteen
years of bad feeling against the Father. The Mother

calls him, and he comes, salt-and-pepper-haired, now, prosperous and bourgeois and wearing sports shirts the Mother would never, not in million years, have allowed him. He strides in, he picks up his Son in his arms, as easily as when he was six years old, and the Son, barely audibly, starts to hum 'Dance for your Daddy'. Everyone, even the case-hardened hospice workers, weeps.

The tumour cannot eat chess, and for as long as the Son can lift the pieces, the Mother plays with him. It induces healthy synaptic activity, say the doctors, and she should keep it up. The doctors do not think the same of *White Fang*, but the Mother reads it aloud anyway. The pathways are there, she thinks, in the brain, for her sledge and its dog. Deep down the brain stem is a pebble which is the Mother and the Son, and this is where they are headed. The pebble is ivory and has an embryo etched on it, curled. 'Speed Bonny Boat', sings the mother to that embryo, and 'You Are My Sunshine'. All those sad songs.

One tumour is an electric storm: it shakes the Son's body like a tree. One tumour picks him up like a pillow and doubles him over and squeezes vomit from him. One tumour sends his eyes back into his skull looking for something. Together, the tumours take him by the throat and he can't swallow.

The Wife returns, with the indefatigable Attila. Attila says they have come to let the truth of the Son's death colour their lives, and the Wife says nothing. The Son's face is frozen now, anyway, so who knows who he knows? The Wife wipes it, and sits by him. All her hairstyles connote innocence, or princess – Rapunzel, Hebe, coronet – and she has grown out of them, all at once, and not noticed.

Days go by. Now the Son's mouth has to be opened with a spatula, wiped with damp cotton wool, dried and greased with Vaseline on a finger, three times an hour. The Mother does this very badly. She worries that his skin will rip, she fears the dry knock of the spatula on bone, she is both too ginger and too clumsy, each time. The Wife does it with Madonna-like ease and the Mother compliments her and she smiles, but still she does not bring the Baby.

More and more of The Saved gather and chant in the Day Room. The Hospice complains, so Attila negotiates duties for them: vase-filling, visiting the unvisited. The Father sits among them, incongruous in his golfing jumper, helping with vases, holding his daughter-in-law's hands, conversing with Attila. He is exactly Attila's height and build, the Mother notes, their heads bend together above all the other heads, the tallest trees. The Father's eyes are constantly wet, he is tireless, he does not mind the spatula at all; the anger, as Attila points out, is all on the Mother's side.

The Mother likes to sit by the Son in the death of the night, when they can be alone. That is when, long after language has started to leave him, she hears the Son say:

'What people forget when they are afraid of dying is that when you die, you are ill. So you don't mind really. Being ill is shit.'

But maybe he didn't really say that. Maybe she has just internalised his response. The last thing he certainly says is 'Big pot', and is probably a request for a bedpan.

The Saved and the Father agree on a plan. The Wife brings the Baby to the Hospice garden. Everyone else disconnects the Son from his tubes and lifts him out of bed, eight pairs of flat, kind hands. Stiff and light as a charred log, they carry him outside and hold him under the cherry tree while the wind blows through it, and chant their mantras, the Father loudest of all on the Oms, while the Wife, a garland on her lovely head, helps the Baby stroke his cheeks with a bunch of blossom. The Mother watches all this from the Hospice window, noting that the Son's expression does not change, longing for the Baby, weeping, thinking she should have been asked.

But, when he does die, it is the Mother beside him. What happens is: he stops breathing and death passes over his body and stills it. The Mother isn't frightened of it, after all. One eye is open, and one shut, and she reaches across and closes the open one. There, now, Jonathon. The eyelid is warm and soft as a silk scarf left in the sun, but there is nothing living now in the hard round of the eyeball, not the least tick or twitch of life.

Then she stands up. Her name is Julia. It is nearly dawn. She goes out to the Day Room where her ex-husband and Attila and The Saved are sleeping, in their white robes, like so many discarded petals. She was going to tell them something, the thing she has learnt, but already it is draining from her, disappearing like water poured over sand, and she lets them sleep on and just sits down.

Moss Witch

Sara Maitland

PERHAPS THERE ARE no more Moss Witches; the times are cast against them. But you can never be certain. In that sense they are like their mosses; they vanish from sites they are known to have flourished in, they are even declared extinct — and then they are there again, there or somewhere else, small, delicate, but triumphant — alive. Moss Witches, like mosses, do not compete; they retreat.

If you do want to look for a Moss Witch, go first to www.geoview.org. Download the map that shows ancient woodland and print it off. Then find the map that shows the mean number of wet days per year. Be careful to get the right map — you do not want the average rainfall map; quantity is not frequency. A wet day is any day in which just one millimetre of rain falls; you can have a high rainfall with fewer wet days; and one millimetre a day is not a high rainfall. Print this map too, ideally on tracing paper. Lay it over the first map. The only known habitations of Moss Witches are in those places where ancient wood-land is caressed by at least two hundred wet days a year. You will see at once that these are not common co-ordinates; there are only a few tiny pockets run-ning down the west coasts of Scotland and Ireland. Like most other witches, Moss Witches have always inhabited very specific ecological niches. So far as we know, and there has been little contemporary research, Moss Witches prefer oak woods and par-ticularly those where over twenty thousand years ago the great, grinding glaciers pushed large chunks of rock into apparently casual heaps and small bright streams leap through the trees. It is, of course, not coincidental that these are also the conditions that suit many types of moss – but Moss Witches are more private, and perhaps more sensitive, than the mosses they are associated with. Mosses can be blatant: great swathes of sphagnum on open moors; little frolicsome tufts on old slate roofs and walls; surprising mounds flourishing on corrugated asbestos; low-lying vel-vet on little-used tarmac roads; and weary, bul-lied, raked and poisoned carpets fighting for their lives on damp lawns. But Moss Witches lurk in the green shade, hide on the north side of trees and make their homes in the dark crevasses of the terminal moraine. If you hope to find a Moss Witch this is where you must go. You must go silently and slowly, waiting on chance and accident. You must pretend you are not searching and you must be patient.

But be very careful. You go at your own peril. The last known encounter with a Moss Witch was very unfortunate.

The bryologist was, in fact, a very lovely young man, although his foxy-red hair and beard might have suggested otherwise. He was lean and fit and sturdy and he delighted in his own company and in solitary wild places. Like many botanists, his passion had come upon him early, in the long free rambles of an unhappy rural childhood, and it never bothered him at all that his peers thought botany was a girly subject and that real men preferred hard things; rocks if you must, stars if you were clever enough and dinosaurs if you had imagination. After taking his degree he had joined an expedition investigating epiphytes in the Peruvian rainforest for a year and had come back filled with a burning ecological fervour and a deep enthusiasm for fieldwork. He was, at this time, employed, to his considerable gratification and satisfaction, by a major European-funded academic research project trying to assess the relative damage to Western European littoral habitats of pollution and global warming. His role was mainly to survey and record Scottish ancient woodlands and to compare the biodiversity of SSSIs with less-protected environments. He specialised in mosses and genuinely loved his subject.

So he came that March morning after a dawn start and a long and lovely hill walk down into a little valley, with a wide shallow river, a flat flood plain and steep sides: glacier carved. Here, hanging on the hillside, trapped between a swathe of ubiquitous Sitka spruce plantation, the haggy reedy bog of the valley floor and the open moor, was a tiny triangle of ancient oak wood with a subsidiary arm of hazel scrub running north. It was a lambent morning; the mist had lifted with sunrise and now shimmered softly in the distance; out on the hill he had heard the returning curlews bubbling on the wing and had prodded freshly laid frogspawn; he had seen his first hill lambs of the year – tiny twins, certainly born that night, their tails wagging their wiry bodies as they burrowed into their mother's udders. He had seen neither human being nor habitation since he had left the pub in the village now seven miles away. He surveyed the valley from above, checked his map and came down from the open hill, skirting the gorse and then a couple of gnarled hawthorns, clambering over the memory of a stone wall, with real pleasure and anticipation. Under the still naked trees the light was green; on the floor, on the trees themselves, on rotted branches and on the randomly piled and strewn rocks – some as big as cottages, some so small he could have lifted them – there were mosses, mosses of a prolific abundance, a lapidary brightness, a soft density such as he had never seen before.

He was warm from his walking; he was tired from his early rising; and he was enchanted by this secret place. Smiling, contented, he lay down on a flat dry rock in the sheltered sunlight and fell asleep.

The Moss Witch did not see him. His hair was the colour of winterkilled bracken; his clothes were a modest khaki green; the sunlight flickered in a light breeze. She did not see him. She came wandering along between rocks and trees and sat down very close to where he slept, crossed her legs, straightened her back and began to sing the spells of her calling, as every Moss Witch must do each day. He woke to that low, strange murmur of language and music; he opened his eyes in disbelief but without shock. She was quite small and obviously very old; her face was carved with long wrinkles running up and down her forehead and cheeks; she was dressed raggedly, in a loose canvas skirt and with thick uneven woollen socks and sandals obviously made from old silage bags. Her woollen jumper was hand-knitted, and not very well. She wore green mittens, which looked somehow damp. He was still sleepy, but when he moved a little and the Moss Witch turned sharply, what she saw was a smiling foxy face and, without thinking, she smiled back.

Tinker? he wondered. Walker like himself though not so well equipped? Gipsy? Mad woman, though a long way from anywhere? He felt some concern and said a tentative 'Hello'.

Even as she did not do so, the Moss Witch knew she should not answer; she should dissolve into the wood and keep her silence. But she was lonely. It had been a very long time. Long, long ago there had been meetings and greetings and gossip among the Moss Witches, quite a jolly social life indeed, with gatherings for wild Sabbats in the stone circles on the hills. There had been more wildwood and more witches then. She could not count the turnings of the world since she had last spoken to anyone and his smile was very sweet. She said 'Hello' back.

He sat up, held out his right hand and said, 'I'm Robert.'

She did not reply but offered her own, still in its mitten. It was knitted in a close-textured stitch and effortlessly he had a clear memory of his mother's swift fingers working endlessly on shame-inducing homemade garments for himself and his sister and recalled that the pattern was called moss stitch and this made him suddenly and fiercely happy. When he shook her hand, small in his large one, he realised that she had only one finger.

There was a silence although they both went on looking at each other. Finally he said, 'Where do you come from?' Even as he asked he remembered the rules in Peru about not trying to interact with people you encountered deep in the jungle. Uncontacted tribes should remain uncontacted, for their own safety, cultural and physical; they had no immunities and were always vulnerable. He shrugged off the thought, smiling again, this time at his own fantasy. There were, after all, no uncontacted tribes in Britain.

'Gondwana, we think; perhaps we drifted northwards,' she said vaguely. ' No one is quite sure about before the ice times; that was the alternate generation, though not of course haploid. But here, really. I've lived here for a very long time.'

He was startled, but she looked so mild and sweet in the dappled green wood that he could not bring himself to admit that she said what he thought she said. Instead, he turned his sudden movement into a stretch for his knapsack, and after rummaging for a moment produced his flask. He unscrewed the top and held it out to her. 'Would you like some water?'

She stretched out her left hand and took the flask from him. Clamping it between her knees, she pulled up her right sleeve and then poured a little water onto her wrist. He stared.

After a pause she said, 'Urgh. Yuck. It's horrible,' and shook her arm vigorously, then bent forward and wiped the splashes delicately from the moss where they had fallen. 'I'm sorry,' she said, 'that was rude, but there is something in it, some chemical thing and I'm rather sensitive... we all are.'

She was mad, he realised, and with it felt a great tenderness – a mad old woman miles from anywhere and in need of looking after. He dreaded the slow totter back to the village, but pushed his irritation away manfully. The effort banished the last of his sleepiness and he got to his feet, pulled out his notebook and pen and began to look around him. Within moments he realised that he had never seen mosses like this; in variety, in luxuriance and somehow in joy. These were joyful mosses and in uniquely healthy condition.

There were before his immediate eye most of the species he was expecting and several he knew instantly were on the Vulnerable or Critically

Endangered lists from the Red Data Book and then some things he did not recognise. He felt a deep excitement and came back to his knapsack. She was still sitting there quite still and seemed ancient and patient. He pulled out his checklist and taxa.

'What are you doing?' she asked him.

'I'm seeing what's here – making a list.'

'I can tell you,' she said. 'I know them all.'

He smiled at her. 'I'm a scientist,' he said. 'I'm afraid I need their proper names.'

'Of course,' she said, 'sit down. I've got 154 species here, not counting the liverworts and the hornworts, of course. I can give you those too. I think I'm up to date although you keep changing your minds about what to call them, don't you? My names may be a bit old-fashioned.'

She chanted the long Latin names, unfaltering.

Leucobryum glaucum. Campylopus pyriformis. Mnium hornum. Atrichum undulatum. Dicranella heteromalla. Bazzania trilobata. Lepidozia cupressina. Colura calyptrifolia. Ulota crispa...

More names than he could have thought of, and some he did not even know. He sat on the rock with his list on his knee, ticking them off as they rolled out of her mouth; there seemed no taxonomic order in her listing, moving from genera to genera along some different system of her own, but her tongue was elegant and nimble around the Latin names. He was both bemused and amused.

Once he stopped her. *Orthodontium gracile,* she sang, and paused smiling. He looked up and she was glancing at him quizzically. 'The slender thread moss.' She looked sly.

'No' he said, 'no, you can't have that here. It grows in the Weald, on the sandstone scarps.'

She laughed. 'Well done,' she said. 'That was a sort of test. But I do have it. Come and see.'

She stood up and beckoned to him; he followed her round a massive granite boulder and up the slope. There behind a hazel thicket and free of the oak trees was a little and obviously artificial heap of sandstone, placed carefully in strata to replicate the scarps of Cheshire and the Weald. And there were two small cushions of *Orthodontium gracile*.

'I like it very much,' she said. 'I like it because it is a bit like me – most people don't know how to see it. It is not as rare as you think. So I invited it in.'

'You mustn't do that,' he said shocked. 'It's protected. You mustn't gather or collect it.'

'No, of course not,' she said. 'I didn't. I invited it.' She smiled at him shyly and went on, 'I think perhaps you and your people are more like *Orthodontium lineare*, more successful but not native.'

Then she sat down and sang the rest of her list.

After that she took his hand in her maimed one and led him down beside the stream which gurgled and sang in small falls and cast a fine mist of spray on the banks where rare mosses and common ferns flourished. He knew then that something strange was happening to him, there in the oak wood, although he did not know what. It was a magical space. It said a lot for his true devotion to bryophytes and his research that he went on looking, that he was not diverted. But time somehow shook itself and came out differently from before – and the space was filled with green, green mosses and her gentle bubbling knowledge. She spoke the language of science and turned it into a love song through her speaking and the mosses sang back the same tune in harmony.

Sometime after noon they came back to where they had started. He was hungry and got out his lunchbox. She sat down beside him.

'Have you got something to eat?' he asked.

'No.'

'Do you want to share mine?'

'I'm non-vascular,' she said. 'I get what I need from the rain. That's why my wrinkles run up and down instead of across. He looked at her face and saw that it was so. She went on, 'And of course it does mean that I revive very quickly even if I do get dried out. That's why I can go exploring, or for that matter,' she looked contented, almost smug, 'sit out in the sun with you.'

None of this seemed as strange to him as it should have seemed. He had reached a point of suspension, open to anything she told him.

'Are you...' but it did not feel right to ask her what she was. He changed the sentence, 'Are you all alone?'

'Yes, sadly,' she said in a matter-of-fact voice. 'I hoped for a long time that I would be monoicous. Nearly half of us are. But no, alas. I'm thoroughly female and as you can imagine that makes things difficult nowadays.' After a little pause she smiled at him, slightly shamefaced, and said in a confessional sort of tone, 'As a matter of fact, that's what happened to my fingers. I was much younger then, of course; I wouldn't try it now, but I did so want a daughter. I thought I might be clonal. You know, I'm not vascular, sensitive to pollution, often misidentified or invisible, all those things; I hoped I might be totipotent as well. So I cut off my fingers and tried to regenerate the cells. But it didn't work. It was a bad mistake. I think we must have been, though, somewhere in the lineage, because of our disjunctions and wide dispersal. That's one of the problems of evolution – losses and gains, losses and gains. Vascular was a smart idea, you have to admit, even at the price of all those vulgar coloured flowers.'

He realised suddenly there were no snowdrops; no green sprouts of bluebells, wild garlic or anemone; no primrose or foxgloves. 'Don't you like flowers?'

'Bloody imperialists,' she replied crossly, 'they invaded, imposed their own infrastructure and ruined our culture, stole our land. And anyway, they're garish – I do honestly prefer the elegance, the subtle beauty of seta, capsules and peristomes.'

He did too, he realised, although he had never thought of it before.

They sat together, contented, in the wildwood, in the space outside of time.

But he lacked her long patience. He could not just sit all day, and eventually he roused himself, shook off the magic, stood up and took out his collecting kit: the little glass bottles with their plastic screw tops, a sharp knife, a waterproof pencil and a squared paper chart.

'What are you doing?' she asked him.

'I'm just going to collect some samples,' he said, 'so we can get them under the microscope.'

'You can't do that.'

'Yes, it's fine,' he said reassuringly. 'I've got a certificate. This is one of the richest sites I've ever seen. We'll get a team in here, later in the year, but

I need some samples now — just to prove it, you know; no one will believe me otherwise.'

'I really cannot let you do that,' she said quietly, still sitting gently on the gentle ground.

But he just smiled kindly at her and moved away up the slope. He bent over a fine little feathered mat: a *sematophyllum* — *S. micans* perhaps; he knelt down, took his knife and scraped along its underside, pulling free its anchoring rhizoids and removing a tiny tuft. He opened one of his bottles, popped in the small green piece and screwed up the top. So she killed him. She was sorry, of course, but for witches it is always duty before pleasure.

Quite soon she knew, with great sadness, that she would have to move on. They would come looking for him and would find her, and rather obviously the crushed skull where she had hit him with the granite rock could not have been an accident.

Later still she realised that she could not just leave his body there. If they found that and did not find her, they might blame some other poor soul, some solitary inhabitant of wood or hill, some vagrant or loner. Someone like her, but not her. Justice is not really an issue that much concerns Moss Witches, but she did not want the hills tramped by heavy-footed policemen or ripped and squashed by quad bikes and 4X4s.

The evening came and with it the chill of March air. Venus hung low in the sky, following the sun down behind the hill, and the high white stars came out one by one, visible through the tree branches. She worked all through the darkness. First she dehydrated the body by stuffing all his orifices with dry sphagnum, more biodegradable than J-cloth and more native than sponge, of which, like all MossWitches, she kept a regular supply for domestic purposes. It sucked up his body fluids, through mouth and ears and anus. She thought too its anti-septic quality might protect her mosses from his contamination after she was gone.

While he was drying out, she went up the hill above the wood and found a ewe that had just given birth and milked it. She mixed the milk with yoghurt culture. She pounded carefully selected ground mosses in her pestle, breaking them down into parts as small as she could manage; she mixed the green ooze with the milk and culture.

When he was desiccated and floppy, she stripped his clothing off, rolled him onto his back among the thick mosses under the rocks and planted him, brushing the cell-rich mixture deep into the nooks and crannies of his body and pulling thicker, more energetic moss clumps over his now cool flesh. At first she was efficient and businesslike, but later she allowed her imagination to cavort. She painted *Aplodon wormskioldii* on his forehead and where his toes poked up through her main planting of *Polytrichum* because it grew on the dead bodies of deer and sheep and might flourish on his bones too. She festooned his genitals with *Plagiochila atlantica* because its little curling fronds were so like the curly mass there. She carried down a rock richly coated with the lichen *Xanthoria parietina* because it was the colour of his foxy hair. She looked at her little arrangement; it was clever, witty even, and secure, but she still felt there was something missing.

After a while she knew. She went round the massive granite boulder and up the slope beyond the oak trees and behind the hazel thicket to her artificial sandstone scarp. There she hacked out one of the cushions of *Orthodontium gracile* on a piece of the reddish rock. Back where he lay, she uncovered his face again, forced his mouth open and placed the sandstone in it, the little moss resting gently on his smiling lips. It was very pleasing to her, because he had been such a sweet man and knew the names of mosses.

Then she spoke clearly and firmly to all the mosses, the liverworts and the lichens she had planted. She told them to grow fast, to grow strong and to grow where she had told them. Bryophytes are not commonly obedient or compliant; they tend to follow theirown rules, coming and going at their own random whim, but she knew this time they would do as she asked because they loved her. Within weeks his body would be part of the moss wood, a green irregular shape among so many others.

Then, sadly, singing all their names one last time, she turned northwards. She climbed high up the hillside and lay down and watched the dawn. When the morning breeze came with first light, she opened her mouth wide and exhaled; and her microscopic spore flowed out between her sixty-four little hydroscopic teeth and was caught by the wind, and carried up into the higher air currents that circulate the earth.

And then... well nobody knows.

Perhaps she blows there still, carried on those upper airs, waiting for a new and quieter time when witches and mosses can flourish.

Perhaps she blew north and west and alighted at last in another small fragment of ancient woodland, a tight ravine leading down to the sea or a small island out beyond the uttermost west, and she lives there still.

Moss witches, like mosses, do not compete; they retreat.

Perhaps there are no more Moss Witches; the times are cast against them. But if you go into ancient woodland and it glows jewel green with moss and is damp and quiet and lovely, then be very careful.

Hitting Trees with Sticks
Jane Rogers

As I am walking home from the shops I pass a young girl hitting a tree. I should say she is about ten years old. She's using a stout stick, quite possibly a broom handle, and she is methodically and repeatedly whacking the trunk, as if it is a job she has to do. There is a boy who stands and watches her. The tree is *Prunus subhirtella*, flowering cherry, growing in the strip of grass that separates the pavement from the dual carriageway.

I know that when I speculate about such things, I am on treacherous ground. But as I look at her I do have a flicker, like the quick opening of a camera shutter, of Henry crouched on the bonnet of the old green Ford, bashing it with a rock. We were at the farm then, so he must have been nine. The flicker is not so much of what he did (because of course I remember the incident perfectly well) as of my own furious older-sister indignation.

Watching the girl today, I feel simply puzzled. So many things are puzzling. The only thing that is certain is that I cannot trust myself to get it right. That flicker of indignant fury runs through my veins like a shot of cognac. Wonderful. I can walk on with a spring in my step. Hitting trees with sticks makes me think of the way they sometimes feed remains of animals to the same species; pigs, for example. Hitting the poor tree with wood, making it beat itself. It is against nature, it adds insult to injury. But maybe I am missing something.

When I come to unlock the front door, I can't find my keys. I find a set of keys in my bag but they aren't mine. Mine have two shiny wooden balls like conkers attached to the key-fob; boxwood and yew, golden and blood red. I've had them for years. They came from trees that were uprooted in the great gale. There is no fob at all with these keys; they are simply attached to a cheap metal ring. I search carefully through my coat pockets and the compartments of my bag. I check in my purse. My own keys are definitely missing – and as for these new ones, I have never seen them in my life before. It is worth trying them, obviously, since they must have appeared in my bag for a reason; and lo and behold, they open my door.

All I can think is that Natalie must have put them there when she had an extra set cut. She must have forgotten, and hung onto the old ones by mistake. I have to have a little chuckle over that, since she's always so keen to point out my lapses of memory.

The post has come while I was out. There's a reminder from the optician, and a letter from the council. Of course, the optician's is right opposite the council offices, so you'd expect that really. Fortunately, my old glasses are still on the table. The council writes about the almond tree. *Your tree which stands 0.5 metres from the neighbouring garden, no 26 Chapel St, is aged and diseased, with consequent danger of falling branches. Our inspector is unable to recommend a preservation order. A tree surgeon will call on Oct 29 to fell this tree and remove the timber. Thank you for your co-operation.* Their thanks are a little premature, since I have no intention of co-operating. I find the whole thing perfectly extraordinary. Last spring the almond tree, *Prunus dulcis*, was smothered in blossom; the petals carpeted the garden like pink snow. I can only assume they've made a mistake. Well, clearly they have made a mistake, because nobody has been to inspect the tree. I'd know if they had because I would have had to let them through the house to get into the garden.

There is always this nagging doubt, however. I have Natalie to thank for that. I know she has my best interests at heart but one can feel undermined. Frankly, one does feel undermined, to the point where I find it safer to tell her very little about my affairs, to save myself the confusion and humiliation of her interference.

I let myself out into the garden to be perfectly sure. It is not a patch on its former glory but there are a few sweet roses still, Rosa Mundi and Madame Alfred Carrière. And at the edge of the lawn the dear little autumn croci, my last present from Neil. Every year they pop up again to astonish and delight, palest mauve against the green. Now, the almond tree. Undoubtedly it is alive: the leaves are turning. There are a couple of bare branches over next door's garden but those leaves may well have dropped early. It might be an idea to take a look. I am in the process of dragging one of the garden chairs to the fence when I hear the doorbell. It rings repeatedly, as if an impatient person were stabbing at it without pause. I have to hasten to the house; there isn't even time to remove my muddy shoes. The doorbell won't survive much more of that treatment.

At the door there's a woman in jeans which are too young and too tight.

'Meals on Wheels. Was you asleep, love?'

'I beg your pardon?'

'Meals on Wheels. Been ringing for the last ten minutes.'

'I think you've made a mistake.'

'Mrs Celia Benson?'

'Yes.'

'Let me bring it in, love, it'll be stone cold.'

'Certainly not.'

'It's your *dinner*, love. Shepherd's pie.'

'There's been a mistake. Is it for number 26? They're away, you know.'

'I'll tell you what, you give your Natalie a ring. She'll remind you. And let me just pop this on the kitchen table.' She pushes her way in and deposits her tray, leaving the kitchen filled with the thick odour of school canteen. Is it possible Natalie has ordered Meals on Wheels without consulting me? Even for Natalie, I think that would be going a little far. What on earth am I supposed to do with it? There'll be some poor old dear somewhere down the road waiting for her dinner, while this sits here getting cold. I should ring Meals on Wheels, I suppose. That will be the best way of clearing up the muddle.

When I go to pick up the phone, it's not in its cradle. Somebody has moved it. Unless, of course, I left it by my bed. That's quite possible, I do take it up with me at night, and I'm not always one hundred per cent about bringing it down again in the morning. You see, I am aware that I'm not perfect at remembering. Painfully aware, you could say. In fact, it's only as I'm making my way upstairs that I remember the girl. There is a girl who stays in the back bedroom. I have a feeling she's not very well, but how she has slept through all this racket I can't imagine. Her door is slightly ajar, so I can peep in without disturbing her. But she's gone. She must have slipped out while I was in the garden. Yes, her bed's empty – she's even made it and pulled up the covers before leaving. She's not a spot of trouble, that girl, she's so quiet and tidy you'd hardly know she was there. I can scarcely remember the last time I spoke to her. My legs are playing up, so I sit on her bed and try to remember; it is important to try. As Natalie says, in her rather brutal way, use it or lose it. I do remember looking in the room just before I went to bed. And she was sleeping then; I saw her dark hair on the pillow. Now I would only have looked in if I was checking she was there, which would suggest, I imagine, that she returned fairly late, after I had eaten and while I was watching television, and that she slipped quietly upstairs without me knowing. It would have been the uncertainty which led me to check on her.

When I stand up and look out of her window, my

eye is drawn to the almond tree. Its leaves are turning, some are yellow and some are red. But there's a suspiciously bare branch above the fence. I hope it's not diseased. Someone has left a garden chair next to it, right on the flower bed. I shall have to go and move it when I've had my dinner. I fancy a cheese salad sandwich, but when I look in the breadbin I am astonished. There is no bread at all, not even a crust! Instead there is a neat brown paper parcel. It looks the sort of parcel that might have been delivered by the postman; brown paper, sellotape, edges neatly folded in. But most curious of all, there is no address. It is much too small to contain bread, so what is it doing in the breadbin? I wonder if I am the victim of some kind of practical joke. Or – I hope I haven't done something foolish. How could this have happened?

Whatever it is, it is important Natalie should not find out; unless, of course, it is another of her attempts to be helpful, backfiring. I have to hunt for the scissors to get through the sellotape; it really is extremely well wrapped. Inside the brown paper is a layer of newspaper, and inside that a layer of bubble wrap. It makes me think of pass the parcel. Imagine my astonishment at discovering inside – my door keys! They are definitely mine; they have the two shiny wooden marbles from the yew and the box; front door, Yale and chub, back door, chub. I am very happy to see them, and I pop them into my coat pocket directly, in order not to mislay them. Then I sit down to my dinner, which is rather cool by this point. I eat half the shepherd's pie but leave the peas. I have never been able to understand the attraction of mushy peas. I can't think why they gave them to me, whoever it was, the person who made my dinner. They have been quick about it, I must say. Tidy too; I wonder if it was the girl upstairs? I could ask Natalie — or perhaps just leave a thank-you note by the cooker; that might be the best plan, cut out the middleman.

I put the kettle on and then I realise the phone is ringing. It is rather difficult to hear when the kettle is roaring away, so I turn it off. Definitely the phone is ringing. But when I go to pick it up somebody has moved it. It isn't in its cradle, it is nowhere to be seen. I look on the table, the dresser, down the arms of the sofa. It has simply vanished. When it stops ringing, I turn the kettle back on and to my annoyance the phone starts up all over again. I have the sudden inspiration that someone may have put it in the breadbin; but no, the breadbin is empty. That in itself is strange, because I must have been shopping this morning. I take the weight off my legs and try to remember what I bought. Bread, obviously, since I have run out; and very likely fruit, because the fruit bowl is empty. I probably bought a nice little piece of cod or chicken for my tea. Where is my shopping? Is it possible someone has nipped in and stolen it? I know that is unlikely. In fact, that is the sort of thing I am quite determined not to think, because it is paranoid, and whilst it is one thing to be forgetful, it is entirely another to be paranoid and irritating to others. As I have said to Natalie, if I ever get like Grandma, shoot me.

All I need to do is apply a little logic. It is almost certain that I have been to the shops, since that is my routine; therefore it is entirely likely that at some point during the afternoon I will come across my shopping. The telephone recommences its ringing and I recall that I have perhaps not fetched it down from beside my bed. I am toiling up the stairs to see, when the doorbell rings.

It is Natalie with her mobile clamped to her ear.

'Why can't you answer the phone, Mum?'

'Why are you phoning me when you're standing on my doorstep?'

'I phoned you from home this morning, and then I phoned you from work. I've been phoning you all day, you never answer. I thought something was wrong.'

'I've been out.'

'Where?' She follows me into the kitchen.

'Shopping.'

'Yes, but you must've come back hours ago. You've had your lunch! What's this?' She picks up a letter and begins to read it. 'Thank God, at last they're dealing with that wretched tree.'

'What does it say?'

'Haven't you read it?'

'I don't believe I have.'

'They're going to chop down the old almond tree that next door keep going on about. You should ask them to chop some other stuff while they're out there; that garden's like a jungle.'

I am not sure who 'they' are, who plan to chop down my tree, but Natalie can be a little impatient so I shall wait till she has gone, then read that letter for myself. I ask her if she would like some tea but she is in a hurry.

'Mum, where's the phone? That's why you didn't answer, isn't it?'

'I don't know what you mean.'

'Where's the phone?' She presses her mobile and the phone begins to ring.

'Please don't do that, Natalie.'

Natalie goes upstairs and after a minute the ringing stops. She comes back down with the phone. 'You need to get an extension. Then you won't have to keep moving it.'

'That's rather an extravagance, isn't it?'

'Mum. I have to come and check on you because you can't answer the phone because you don't know where it is. If buying another phone stops that from happening, won't it make life easier for the both of us?'

'There really isn't any need for you to check on me, you know.'

Natalie opens the fridge. 'What are you having for tea?'

'Chops.'

'Where are they?'

'I haven't unpacked my shopping yet.'

She sits down at the table. 'Look, I worry about you. You forget things. I know you want to be independent but sometimes –'

'What do you want me to do?'

'Get another phone. I'll get it for you. You can pay me back. Alright?'

'Alright.'

'Good. Shall I unpack your shopping before I go?'

'It's fine, thank you. I can do it myself.'

'OK. I'll call in tomorrow after work. See you, Mum.' She kisses me and lets herself out. Lucky about that shopping; now, I have to find it, quick sticks, before it slips my mind again. I have an inkling I've put it in the breadbin – but no. It isn't in the fridge or the cooker; I wonder if the girl upstairs has taken it to her room by mistake? But a thorough search upstairs draws a blank. I have to sit on her bed for a little rest; I really am feeling quite done in.

When I come back down to the kitchen, I notice a letter from the council on the table. They want to cut down the almond tree! It was here when Neil and I bought this house in 1951. It must be nearly as old as I am. I should be very sad to see it go. But I must concentrate on the shopping. I might have left it in the garden. My legs are painful and it seems to me that the joy has rather gone out of the day. Maybe I could go to bed early and not bother with tea.

No, that would not be sensible. It is important to have a routine. Break your routine and where are you? Adrift on a wide, wide sea. I let myself out into the garden; it is already dusk, with a chill in the air. Someone has left one of the garden chairs on the flower bed near the tree. I move it, and then I have a good look under the bushes for my shopping. If it isn't there it's nowhere; and that's what I am forced to conclude. That shopping has vanished. It is a relief to feel certain about it. At least now I can sit down in the warm and stop worrying. But when I try to go back inside, the door won't budge. I know I haven't locked it. I check my pockets – no keys. That proves it. But it is definitely locked. I sit on a garden chair and try to decide what to do. Who has locked me out? Whoever has done it might well be a robber; might, even at this moment, be going through my things. I peer into the sitting room but it is too dark to see.

Well, if there is a robber, let him take what he wants and go. My main concern is that Natalie shouldn't know what has happened. But how am I to get out of the garden? I can hardly stay here all night! I wonder if the girl upstairs has come in. I knock on the back door, then tap on the sitting-room window. There is no reply. Then I hear the phone begin to ring. I hope she might answer it, but it rings and rings, more than twenty times. Who could be ringing me? Natalie. I am decidedly chilly. I feel around in the blackness of the garden shed and manage to lay my hands on the picnic cloth, which I wrap around my shoulders. It's an old Indian bedspread; there's not a lot of warmth in it, but it smells rather sweetly of grass clippings. The outdoor broom topples over, so I take it for a walking stick. I hobble back to the sitting-room window and listen to the phone ringing again. I expect she will come round in a while. She will be cross with me.

I don't want to be any trouble and everything seems to conspire against it. I can see I am nothing but trouble. Perhaps I can make them hear me next door. But when I look up at their house, I remember they're away. They leave that bright bathroom light on to fool robbers, though any robber worth his salt wouldn't take long to work out that the bathroom light has been left on for a fortnight. They think nothing of wasting electricity; the bulb must be 200 watts. It shines straight down onto my almond tree, as if it were the star of the stage. That tree has been nothing but trouble.

When Natalie comes, she'll not only be cross about the phone, she'll also be cross about the tree. It has been diseased for years. If it wasn't for that tree I would never have had to come into the garden in the first place. The trouble it's caused: the letters, the telephone calls, the stream of people coming and going about that tree: it is extraordinary. Why can't they just chop it down and have done with it?

I am a patient woman, I believe I am. I try to be patient. Not like Henry; he always had a horrible temper on him. I can see him now, hitting and hitting that old green Ford, just because they wouldn't let him ride the tractor. But I have to ask where it has got me. Look at me now, trapped in my own garden in the cold and the dark, with my swollen legs really quite troublesome, having to face Natalie being angry with me yet again. Natalie is angry. *I* should be angry. First Grandma, and now this. I have to wonder, you know; is she me? Am I my mother?

I think about being angry. I think about feeling a hot flicker of rage, coursing through my veins like a shot of cognac. I think I *am* angry. Really, I have had enough of all this, I have had it up to here. Grasping the garden broom firmly, I stride over to that wretched tree. It's time I taught it a lesson. I raise my broom and begin to whack it, good solid ringing blows on the trunk. Yes! My anger is warming me through and through. It is time that old tree knew it was beaten.

Exchange Rates
Lionel Shriver

WHEN ELLIOT FIRST heard that his father was coming
to London he was anxious, but the single dinner the
visit boiled down to went harmlessly enough. It was
the tiny financial footnote to the occasion that had
repercussions.

Keen to select a profoundly British venue, Elliot
had arranged to meet his father at a funky gastro-
pub on The Cut, a street name that itself embodied
his adoptive country's quirky nomenclatural charm.
(Elliot collected oddball street names. A recent
business trip to Beverley had netted the beguiling
byways 'Old Waste' and 'North Bar Within'. The
penchant was an economy. A collection of Victorian
teapots, say, would run to thousands of quid; street
names were free.) The Anchor & Hope was within

walking distance of his Bermondsey flat, but the slog was just long enough to discourage his father from strolling back for coffee to discover that his son, at the humiliating age of 43, was living with room-mates like some scraping grad student. His father wouldn't understand that single adults with full-time jobs teaming up to share a flat was commonplace in this city, where in Elliot's conversation the adjectives exorbitant, larcenous and extortionate had grown impotent from overuse.

Still, while straining to read the specials on the chalk board, Elliot's father Harold Ivy, though a retired history professor whose specialty was seventeenth-century England, didn't wax eloquent on how the Thames once froze so solid that merchants sold their wares in 'frost fairs' on its surface. No, he couldn't stop talking about what everything cost. Like every American who'd visited Elliot in London the last few years, Harold remarked in indignation on the fact that, while the exchange rate was 2:1, a pound and a dollar bought roughly the same thing. 'This "baby beet-leaf salad" with duck "shreds",' Harold pointed. '£8 – that's $16! In a bar! For an appetizer!'

'They'd call it a "starter".' Elliot felt at once responsible for the prices, and proud of himself for surviving them. In his head, he now routinely doubled the cost of British goods into dollars, to heighten the outraged sticker-shock; on visits back home, he halved $18.99 into pounds to make the new REM CD seem cheerfully cheap.

'It's not just restaurants, it's everything,' Harold fumed. 'When I was in Oxford making some last-minute notes on my guest lecture, my roller-ball went dry. I pick up a little packet of three at a stationer's – £6! That's $4.00 apiece!'

'Welcome to my world,' said Elliot. 'There are only two bargains in the UK: marmalade and breakfast cereal. Meanwhile, everyone here is taking buying-binge trips to New York. They think everything is half-price.'

'Never mind a few shopping sprees, I don't know why the population of Britain doesn't pick up and move wholesale to the United States. We may have an idiot president, but at least you don't have to take out a second mortgage to buy a sandwich.'

Harold opined about how relieved he was that Oxford was covering his London overnight, especially once he got a look at the hotel's rates. 'Still,' he added, puffing up a bit, 'they put your old dad in some pretty fancy digs! Lavender-whatnot shampoo, heated towel racks. And carte blanche on the mini-bar! Feels good to be on expenses again.'

There was a note in his father's voice that Elliot

would only retrieve weeks later, but at the time he was distracted by the image of Harold stuffing all the chic hotel toiletries into his luggage, and washing his hands with plain water so he didn't have to unwrap the soap, the better to spirit the booty back home. Maybe he'd even remember to haul back a swag-bag of Rose's thin-cut lemon-lime and Weetabix.

Naturally Elliot joined his cheapskate father in declining to order a starter, and a full bottle of wine was out of the question. It went without saying as well that they'd skip dessert. This had always been the form when eating out with his parents: one main course, tap water, *maybe* a glass of wine if they were feeling extravagant, and then the bill, ensuring that at least these oppressively scrimping occasions were short.

It wasn't that Elliot didn't like his father, a vigorous 73 with a full head of knurling white hair that gave Elliot hope for his own unruly mop in future. Granted, the guy's having put on some serious weight in the last few years was concerning; the elderly – a word that Elliot applied to his father with something between unease and consternation – were prone to becoming bizarrely obsessed with food. Nevertheless, amidst the student body his father's passion for 'the *real* Civil War' had been famously infectious, and he still pronounced commandingly on issues of the day as if the whole world were perched on the edge of its collective chair, waiting to hear the verdict from Professor Ivy. Teaching conferred the arbitrary yet absolute authority of tin-pot dictatorships, and was bound to go to anyone's head eventually. Besides, Elliot was glad that his father hadn't slid into the passive apathy of many pensioners, who take refuge in bewilderment, or who revel in a grim satisfaction that the likes of climate change and desertification would wreak their worst destruction on someone else. Harold Ivy had retired from Amherst; he had not retired from the planet.

No, the trouble was Elliot's sense of filial inadequacy, made doubly shameful for being trite. Harold didn't condescend to his younger son exactly, and Elliot hated to think that he might still be yearning for his father's approval (though he probably was). It was more that Elliot's life didn't *interest* his father much. While his father had been bent on scholarship from freshman year at Princeton, Elliot had never enjoyed a strong sense of occupational calling. After an aimless major in history at Brandeis that in retrospect was sycophantic, he'd co-founded a catering company that went bankrupt after a client sued over an *alleged* food-poisoning incident. He'd taught English to unsalvageables in South Boston; when one of his own students held him up at knife-point, he'd rebelled against thankless do-gooding for next to nothing, and spent three years in middle-management with AT&T – unsurprisingly, as boring as it sounds. Making the mistake of many of his fellow seekers in the same department at Boston U, he began a Masters in clinical psychology under the illusion that the aim was to sort out his own confusions, rather than for an assured, well-adjusted graduate to sort out the confusions of someone else. Little matter, since he aborted his second year, having fallen hard and helplessly for a sly, sarky British tourist he'd met at the Plough in Cambridge – the copy-cat Cambridge – who was heading home to London the following month.

Personally, Elliot could see a pattern: a pendulum swing between finding meaning and making money. But that structure had to be imposed on a narrative that to his father was simply incoherent. In Harold Ivy's terms, about the only half-intriguing thing that Elliot had ever done was move to the UK, although the initial motivation – to marry Caitlin, who was from Barnes – didn't seem quite respectable for a guy. Elliot did feel that he'd found his professional footing at last; everyone at the engineering society for which he worked said he was a natural at events planning. But his father could never come up with anything to ask about his job. Harold's idea of proper 'events planning' was preparation for the Battle of Hastings.

Fortunately, their single course of wild boar and salsify stew (not altogether distinguishable from pork roast and parsnips) was readily occupied with family news – his mother's successful hip replacement, his brother's latest coup (a big commission to install solar panels on a public library; it was irksome how Robert managed to conceal with a cloak of virtue that he was really just a salesman), and an awkward inquiry about how was Caitlin, to which Elliot was obliged to reply that he had no idea. Harold pored over the bill before paying in cash. Elliot didn't need to see the print-out to be sure that the tip was puny.

'By the way,' Harold appended, pulling several £20 notes from his wallet. 'You know, I'm flying back to Logan tomorrow morning. But just to keep the bureaucracy down, Oxford paid my honorarium in cash. No use to me in Massachusetts, and I've got most of it left. I stopped in a bank, and they charge a £5 commission – ten bucks! That seemed like throwing money away. I thought, since you must spend sterling all the time…'

Elliot cheered, and mentally retracted his unkind exasperation at his father's parsimonious approach to dining out. It looked like well over £100 – not enough to have an improving effect on his thus-far apocryphal property deposit, but a little extra pocket money never went amiss. He'd just arranged a surprised-but-grateful expression when his father kept talking.

'And you still have an American bank account, right? So I thought you could change the money for me, and I could skip paying that ridiculous fee.'

Elliot's face twitched from surprised-but-grateful to plain surprised. 'Well, I don't have any dollars on me...'

'That's okay, just slip a cheque in the mail.' Harold counted the bills. 'I make that £160. Don't worry, I trust you. No receipt required!'

'Yes, but do you trust me not to charge you a £5 fee?'

The humour felt strained. When they parted outside, Elliot's ludicrously elaborate instructions for how to get to the tube stop at Waterloo right around the corner were meant to cover for an abrupt irritability. The evening felt spoilt, and when he hugged his burly father goodbye, his heart wasn't in it. He'd remember the embrace later: its inattention, its merely gesturing back pat, the tense, lopsided twist of his own insincere smile.

Hunching home, hands jammed in his pockets,

Elliot considered why, exactly, his father using his son as a *bureau de change* was quite so annoying. Since exchange rates were always rigged in the bank's favour, he himself maintained a hard-and-fast policy of never changing currencies. Modest birthday and Christmas cheques from his parents (they wouldn't spring for the postage on presents) and commercial rebates from his own spending sprees Stateside (no one but a moron bought a computer in the UK) he always deposited in his Boston Citibank account, which also held his savings from that lucrative stint with AT&T. Especially since the value of American currency had plummeted – Britons now regarded a dollar as a small green rectangle for wiping one's bum – he wasn't about to effectively halve its buying power by transferring his precious $37K-and-change to NatWest. Instead, he was hoarding his few spare pounds for a deposit on a flat. And now he was expected to do on his father's account what he never, ever did on his own: trade dollars for pounds.

Moreover, his father doubtless expected Elliot to pony up the exchange rate quoted on the evening news: recently, about $1.97 to the pound, give or take. But peons didn't get anywhere near $1.97 at banks, whose exchange rates' relation to the currency market was capricious to nonexistent. At

NatWest, his father would have been lucky to get $1.85. Instead, Elliot would be expected to write his father a cheque for $320 – rounding up the rate to a tidy 2:1.

All right, it wasn't that much money. Yet there was a principle at stake. On however miniature a scale, his own father was taking advantage of him, all in the interests of saving five miserable pounds. Elliot wasn't too clear on the details, but Harold Ivy's financial circumstances had to be healthy. If nothing else, his parents owned their own home, free and clear, which they had bought in the sane era when a house was still a normal acquisition purchased by normally salaried people that they paid off in a normal timeframe of perhaps twenty years. These days even a poky two-bedroom walk-up in a dubious 'transitional neighbourhood' had become an unimaginable luxury that lowly wage-earners like himself would only own outright by toiling at two jobs until age 152. As for a proper *house*, well, that was a farcical pipe dream, like a private trip to the moon, within the means only of lottery winners, Arab sheiks, Russian oil oligarchs and City of London shysters.

Hunkering down Webber Street, Elliot glared at the smug yellow-bricked terraces with their vain, prissy white curtains and self-congratulatory flower pots. Before moving to Britain, it had never been his reigning ambition to own property. Nevertheless, he'd lived for eleven years amidst a real-estate frenzy of historically unprecedented proportions, and he felt left out. All around him people were making fortunes by flipping one little dump after another, and meantime he was numbly forking out £800 a month for a single room (okay, the largest room) of a shared three-bedroom, and he felt like a sucker. For all its post-class pretensions, modern Britain was just as feudally cleaved into serfs and landowning gentry as in the Middle Ages, and entering his own middle age Elliot was still a serf. Gleaming brass escutcheons seemed to be locking Elliot Ivy personally out, while walls on either side of the road gloated, rising implacably against this poor asshole American who hadn't the brains to have swung onto the much-vaunted 'housing ladder' when he'd had the chance. Now the end of that ladder was dangling a hundred feet in the air, and all the slaphappy home-owners carousing on the bottom rung were pointing down at him and cackling.

It was all his parents' fault.

Throughout his upbringing they'd pinched their pennies – buying single-ply toilet roll with its notorious 'poke-through' problem, clothing Elliot in Robert's hand-me-downs and foreswearing air-conditioning, which meant that his friends would boycott his house all summer. Made from quick-sale vegetables with their ignominious yellow stickers, stir-fry suppers had exuded the faint ammoniated whiff of mushrooms gone slippery. Less from necessity than catechism, his mother never bought herself a dress at Filene's Basement that wasn't 'on sale'. As much as he resisted such joyless thrift in theory, like it or not, the tightwad gene was buried deep in his own DNA, and these days at Iceland Elliot bought single-ply, too.

The year he'd moved to London Elliot had no reason to know would prove a watershed, and not because Labour had come to power. In hindsight (though, of course, making decisions 'in hindsight' everyone would be rich), he should have urged Caitlin to sell her flat, that they might embark on married life in a new home that they had bought together. Back then, he might easily have transferred his Citibank savings (during a now-nostalgic era of exchange rates sometimes as low as $1.40) to go 50-50 on a deposit. Instead, with the accommodating deference of a stranger in a strange land, he'd contributed his half of her mortgage payments for four years, during which Caitlin's flat nearly doubled in value. It was news to him when they split that all along he hadn't been building a share in the escalating equity, but, the initial pittance of a deposit being Caitlin's, paying 'rent'. Bitterness was never an attractive quality, but on this point – the monies at issue running to about £55K, more than enough to have set him up in his own place – Elliot was well and truly bitter. The real test wasn't how they dealt with illness, whether they were 'supportive' or sexually faithful; you only discovered what anyone was made of once on the pointy end of how they handled money.

In hindsight, too, as soon as he gave up on the marriage (Caitlin was under the deluded impression that she had kicked him out), he should again have availed himself of his American savings to purchase the first crappy little dive that he could snag. But by that point, British property was already to his mind wildly overvalued. Fatally, then, he had rented the flat in Bermondsey with two workmates and resolved to sit tight. Since then, property had appreciated another staggering 60 per cent. Would his mother be dismayed, or gratified? Elliot had been waiting in vain for houses to go 'on sale'.

As he trooped up Pilgrimage and rounded on Manciple Street (both street names long ago added to his collection), even the blocks of ex-council flats seemed to be sneering with schoolyard contempt, 'We were bought before 1997, *nyah*-nyah-*nyah*-nyah-*nyah*-nyah!' Since one couldn't walk any distance in this city without passing by residential dwellings, even brief scuttles home like this one wore him out with resentment.

Unlocking the front door of his shared loft conversion on Long Lane, Elliot supposed morosely that he could always go back to the States. When asked by uncomprehending Brits why he stayed in this bleak, godforsaken country, he would often promote some twaddle about 'culture', but the truth was closer to 'furniture'. In an ostentatious display of sexually liberated largesse that helped to cover for some tiny trace of embarrassment over screwing him on the flat, Caitlin had made a great show of dividing the appointments they'd bought together strictly down the middle. Thus he was possessed of a handsome 200-year-old dining table whose rugged, manly cut he quite fancied. Currently the social centre of the loft, it was a heavy walnut affair that expanded to seat eight – too massive to ship, too cherished to abandon. He could see himself living in this city for the rest of his life, manacled to the legs of that walnut dining table.

Besides, taunted by those fatuous facades of self-satisfied brick, buffeted by the hostile forces of $4 roller-balls, Elliot did not want to admit defeat.

Typically, his father's £160 quickly frittered from

Elliot's wallet on dull rubbish. He may have treated himself to a couple of proper lunches instead of meagrely filled M&S Chicken Fajita Wraps, but otherwise lost the packet to new batteries for the Long Lane radio-controlled thermostat, Sainsbury's thievingly priced non-bio laundry detergent because he couldn't be bothered to go all the way to Lidl, a shocking dry-cleaning bill… in all, to the kind of expenditures at the end of which life is no better and you have nothing that you didn't have before.

Now that the money was spent and he still had to write his father a cheque, Elliot experienced a fresh burst of exasperation. Wouldn't it have been more *gracious* for Harold to have simply given his son the cash? Did the guy really need $320 – a *rounded-up* $320? The folderol now required was hardly worth five quid: writing the cheque, addressing the envelope, and queuing the usual 45 minutes for an airmail stamp at one of London's few remaining post offices, now that Britain considered post offices the same outlandish luxury as houses.

More importantly, didn't this amount of bother to save a fiver epitomize all that was wrong with his parents? His father's pettiness at the Anchor & Hope mirrored the killjoy stinting that had tyrannized Elliot's boyhood. Store-brand white bread bought in 2lb. loaves, a fraction cheaper per weight than the

1lb. size, had guaranteed that the sandwiches in his second week's brown-bag school lunches would be stale, with spots of mould pinched off the crusts. The kitchen drawers of his childhood were eternally cluttered with the tat of Green Stamps and ten-cent-off coupons for Tang. On phone calls with his grandparents, he and Robert had been distracted by sharp reminders to 'keep it short' because the call was – always iterated in hushed, reverential tones – 'long distance'. Now all his grandparents were dead. How was that for *long distance?*

As it happened, while Elliot foot-dragged on returning Harold's honorarium in dollars, the pound slumped to its lowest rate in years, and was now trading in the markets at $1.78. Deteremined to teach his father a lesson, although he may have been a little hazy about what lesson, he popped into NatWest on his way to work. The bank was selling dollars at the predictably less generous rate of $1.69. Back home at his desk that night, Elliot punched the numbers into his calculator: £160 wasn't worth anywhere near $320, but $270.40. In a fit of exactitude, before writing a cheque for the amount to the penny, he subtracted another $1.27 – the 75p for an airmail stamp.

Thus a week later an e-mail arrived in Elliot's personal

gmail account from prof.harold.ivy@aol.com,whose subject-line read, 'Miscalculation?' Its text was terse and lacked a greeting: 'got the check. seems a bit short. 160 pounds = $269.13????????'

This response was strangely satisfying. It wasn't like his father, a stickler for grammatical correctness even in this conventionally slapdash medium, to fail to capitalize or to omit the subjects of his sentences. The juvenile profusion of question marks was also not in keeping with Harold Ivy's commonly restrained style, and indicated that the message – whatever that was – had struck home.

Lingering over his reply with a glass of merlot that evening, Elliot assumed the same tutorial tone to which he himself had been subjected during countless instructional dinners as a boy. He patiently explained about the currency market, and how the rates in the *Boston Globe's* financial pages were not remotely representative of exchange rates on the high street here in London. He noted that the pound had recently dipped, alas in this instance to Harold's disadvantage. He rued with light-hearted despair that UK postage was 'far more dear' – a pleasingly British way of putting it – than the US mail; hence the deduction of $1.27. Signing off with an allusive flourish, Elliot typed, 'Welcome to my world', and hit *send*.

Yet when he received no reply over the following several days, Elliot's sense of triumph rapidly ebbed to an odd, curiously tormenting hollowness. And then the phone rang.

Elliot knew something was wrong as soon as he heard his mother's voice. Though industry deregulation had radically cheapened the international phone call, Bea Ivy was still averse to 'long distance', and was wont to communicate with e-mails that were long, chatty and free. Too, unless she'd got so scatty as to forget the five-hour time difference, she must have realized that in London it was 4am.

Impressively practical and matter-of-fact, his mother delivered the end of the world as she knew it: 'I'm so sorry to have to tell you this, and I know it will come as a shock. His last check-up gave him the all-clear. But shortly after dinner tonight, your father had a heart attack. I just came back from the hospital. As far as I could tell, the doctors did everything they could. But Elliot...' The line rustled for a second or two with static. 'Your father didn't make it.'

Of course, she suffered bouts of weeping. But Bea also inhabited moments of repose, one of which descended during the memorial gathering back at the house in Amherst after the funeral.

'I'm so relieved that you saw your father in London last month,' she told Elliot, politely accepting a skewer of chicken satay proffered by the catering staff, then disposing of it discreetly on the mantel. 'In a way, you got to say goodbye.'

'In a way,' said Elliot wearily, remembering that they had squandered a goodly proportion of that evening on Britain's high prices.

'And I'm especially grateful that Harold got that opportunity to speak at Oxford. I can't tell you how much that invitation meant to him. I suppose I tried to shelter you from his moodiness. You have your own life, in such a big, exciting city, where you're out on the town all the time – I *hope* looking for a young woman with better taste than that Caitlin.' To his mother, his ex was always *that Caitlin*, a syntax she may have picked up from Bill Clinton.

'Well, my life in London is hardly one big party,' said Elliot, whose demeanour since hearing the news had been not only stricken, but hangdog.

'Anyway, these last five years have been – were pretty hard for your father. He was used to being so busy, flying off to academic conferences all over the world. Always working on a paper after dinner, or drafting a new curriculum. Unlike most of the faculty, Harold didn't give the same set lectures over and over. He was always refining, doing new research and polishing his ideas. Then, retirement – it just didn't sit well with him. He'd never been a potterer. He had no interest in the garden, or in doing frivolous, time-filling things like taking a class in Indian cooking. He'd read, but even reading wasn't the same. He was used to reading for a reason.'

'You mean he was depressed.'

'I suppose that's what you'd call it. The phone rarely rang, and some days he got no e-mails at all. At Amherst, he used to complain so about being inundated, about how e-mails had become a plague! But, you know, be careful what you wish for.'

'He still got a few e-mails,' said Elliot heavily.

'So I was thrilled when they asked him to speak in Oxford – the cradle of his sacred dictionary! It was such a compliment, since obviously the British have plenty of historians who specialize in seventeenth-century England in their own country. When the invitation came in, it changed his whole... Well, he was back to his old self.'

'Yeah, he did seem pretty energized when we had dinner.' For the first time, Elliot realized that he'd never asked his father what his lecture had been about.

'It wasn't only the invitation. Being flown across the Atlantic again, at someone else's expense. A hotel, being wined and dined. Even getting an honorarium, when he used to be paid to speak all the time. Oh, I don't think the college paid him all that much. Oxford doesn't have nearly as much money to throw around as our well-endowed Ivy League, I don't need to tell you that! Still, to finally earn something again, instead of just drawing down a pension...'

Feeling a little sick, Elliot deposited his smoked-salmon canapé next to the satay skewer on the mantel.

'I think too little is made of the satisfaction of earning money,' said his mother philosophically. 'I discovered it myself only when I started doing that freelance editing, and then I kicked myself for not having brought in a bit of my own income a long time before. Oh, it was only part-time, and we didn't especially need the extra money. But I loved the way those checks in the mail made me *feel*. I was worth something, literally worth something, in terms that other people take seriously. We make such a fuss over the joy of spending. But I think *earning* money is a much richer experience than buying some new trinket. Your father certainly felt the same. When I finally started working myself, I was even a little piqued, as if Harold should have let me in on the secret. As if all along, instead of generously supporting our family, he'd been selfishly indulging a private pleasure.'

Though her self-possession under the circumstances was remarkable, Bea couldn't have been so
coolly collected that she was feigning innocence;
clearly his father had kept his irritation at the light
Citibank cheque to himself. But successfully burying
the episode only made Elliot feel worse.

Glumly accepting a third glass of wine and already
planning on a fourth, Elliot rehearsed the evening at
the Anchor & Hope. Why, he'd simply taken it for
granted that his father would pay the bill. That's what
parents did. But he was 43, with a full-time job, not
some teenager saving for a motorbike by flipping
burgers. Would it have killed him to have treated his
father to a meal in Elliot's own city? Astonishingly, he
could not recall once eating out with his parents and
picking up the tab. He had never taken his own father
out to dinner, and now he never would.

Making a mental subtraction whose difficulty
suggested that a fourth glass of wine was a bad idea,
Elliot calculated that in giving his father the 'real'
exchange rate instead of rounding up to 2:1, he had
saved himself the princely sum of $50.87.

Maybe the problem really was genetic.

There had been a peculiar resolution about his
mother after the funeral, a firm sense of direction
that had seemed to Elliot premature at the time. His

parents' marriage of 48 years had been close, and he wouldn't have expected her to achieve this forward-looking determination half so quickly. But he had misinterpreted her sense of purpose. It wasn't that unusual, when the marriage was sound: within a handful of weeks, she died.

Thus, after the wheels of probate had finished turning, he and Robert were settled with an inheritance far more sizable that Elliot would ever have anticipated.

Once the money landed in Citibank, he didn't visualize it as rows of zeros, stacks of banded bills, or bars of gold bullion. Rather, he pictured a tat of Green Stamps and ten-cent-off coupons for Tang; mounds of mildewing discount dresses, mountains of moulding store-brand white bread and teetering towers of toilet roll – single-ply. Rotting somewhere in a vault in Boston were hundreds, perhaps thousands of unordered starters, foregone desserts and undrunk cups of restaurant coffee. And it was freezing in there – icy with 48 summers' worth of air-conditioning that his parents had lived without.

With however poor an exchange rate, Elliot could now readily purchase a respectable home in London – where during a vertiginous economic downturn property prices had finally started to slide, and it might indeed be possible, he thought wanly, to find a house 'on sale'. Toward this end, he could not only apply his inheritance, the nest-egg in pounds at NatWest and his original American savings of $37K-and-change, but an outstanding cheque for $269.13, which had never been cashed.

Biographical Notes

NAOMI ALDERMAN'S first novel, *Disobedience* was released in 2006 and won the Orange Award for New Writers. The *Jewish Tribune* called the novel a 'gross contribution to the realms of sordid literature'.

In 2007 Naomi was named *Sunday Times* Young Writer of the Year, and one of Waterstones' 25 Writers for the Future. Naomi also writes online computer games, including writing for Penguin's award-winning We Tell Stories project. Penguin will publish her new novel, *The Lessons*, in April 2010.

KATE CLANCHY was born in Glasgow in 1965 and was educated in Edinburgh and Oxford. She is a popular poet: her collections, *Slattern, Samarkand* and *Newborn*, have brought her many literary awards including a *Somerset Maugham Award* and *Saltire* and *Forward Prizes*. She writes frequently for Radio 4 and comment for the Guardian. Her latest book, *Antigona and Me*, was published in hardback under the title *What Is She Doing Here?* It was dramatised on BBC Radio 4, won the *Writers' Guild Award* for *Best Book 2008* and was shortlisted for the *Scottish Mortgage Investment Trust Book Award 2009*, in partnership with the *Scottish Arts Council*.

SARA MAITLAND was born in 1950. Her first novel *Daughter of Jerusalem* won the Somerset Maugham Award in 1979. Since then she has written five more novels and has published five collections of short stories, including *On Becoming a Fairy Godmother* (Maia Press 2003). In March 2008 Maia press published *Far North and other dark tales* to celebrate the launch of the film "Far North", directed by Asif Kapadia and starring Michelle Yeoh and Sean Bean, based on that dark tale.

In 2004 she moved to Galloway and built herself a house on the moors above New Luce. *A Book of Silence*, (Granta 2008) is partly a cultural history of silence and partly a personal memoir of her own search of that elusive lifestyle. She is currently working on a book about forests and fairy stories.

MossWitch first appeared in *When it Changed* edited by Geoff Ryman (Comma Press, 2009)

JANE ROGERS has written eight novels including *Mr Wroe's Virgins* (which she dramatised as a BBC TV serial); *Promised Lands,* (Writers' Guild Best Novel Award 1996); Island (1999, Arts Council Writers Award, currently in development as a film); and *The Voyage Home* (2004). She also writes for radio, most recently *Dear Writer* (Afternoon Play) and an adaptation of *The Age of Innocence* for Classic Serial. Her short stories have been broadcast on radio and occasionally published, most recently by Comma Press. She has also edited Oxford University Press' *Good Fiction Guide*. She is currently working on some short stories, and on a Classic Serial adaptation of *The Custom of the Country.*

She is Professor of Writing at Sheffield Hallam University, and Course Leader in Writing at the Open College of the Arts.

www.janerogers.org

LIONEL SHRIVER is best known for the *New York Times* bestseller *The Post-Birthday World* (2007) and the international bestseller *We Need to Talk About Kevin*, the 2005 Orange Prize winner that has now sold over a million copies worldwide. Her work has been translated into 25 different languages. She is a widely published journalist, appearing regularly in the *Guardian*, the *Sunday Times*, the *Economist*, and the *Wall Street Journal*, among many other publications. Her ninth novel, *So Much for That*, will be released in March 2010.